Praise for the novels of Timothy Watts . . .

The Money Lovers

"Slick and sexy." —*New York Times Book Review*

"Terrific . . . Watts is Elmore Leonard with a nasty attitude."
—**Stephen Solomita**

"A superior thriller that plays the angles just right."
—*Seattle Times*

"An appealing noir-flavored story of one backstab after another." —*San Francisco Chronicle*

"Favorable comparisons with Elmore Leonard are unavoid-
able . . . The dialogue is hip without being obvious, the tension
is palpable, and the ending is a satisfying double-clutch."
—*Booklist*

Cons

"Heart-stopping suspense . . . [a] masterpiece."
—*Philadelphia Inquirer*

"Precision tuned . . . purrs with professionalism."
—*New York Times Book Review*

"Seductive . . . worthy of Jim Thompson or James Crumley."
—*Publishers Weekly*

"An impressive debut. Watts has talent to spare."
—*Kirkus Reviews*

Feeling Minnesota

A NOVEL BY TIMOTHY WATTS

BASED ON THE SCREENPLAY BY STEVEN BAIGELMAN

BOULEVARD BOOKS, NEW YORK

FEELING MINNESOTA

A Boulevard Book / published by arrangement with
New Line Productions, Inc.

PRINTING HISTORY
Boulevard trade paperback edition / March 1996

The Putnam Berkley World Wide Web site address is
http://www.berkley.com

ISBN: 1-57297-115-0

BOULEVARD
Boulevard Books are published by The Berkley Publishing Group,
200 Madison Avenue, New York, New York 10016.
BOULEVARD and its logo are trademarks
belonging to Berkley Publishing Corporation.

PRINTED IN THE UNITED STATES OF AMERICA

10 9 8 7 6 5 4 3 2 1

Prologue

MINNESOTA 1972

IT FELT LIKE HOT acid dripping into raw flesh, as if his arm was going to shrivel up and fall off. The pain was so intense that it seemed to be alive, a thing that breathed, had a mind of its own, and moved with white-hot precision, a musical band wildly out of tune, marching across his nerve endings, dragging sharp-cleated shoes.

Screaming did nothing.

He'd been in the other room, sitting wide-eyed and waiting for his life, as it had been up until today, to end. There was music floating through the air. It sounded scratchy, as if the singer had covered his mouth with tinfoil and tried to sing through it. A dried-up, faraway, tinny tone like those old 78 rpm records. Every once in a while the needle would skip, and it would sound like the singer was trying to play catch-up to the music.

The phonograph was in the far corner of the room, by the

1

one window that was clean enough to let a dusty ray of late-afternoon sunlight in. There was a worn, oval throw rug on the floor that might have been white at one time but had turned an unremarkable gray through time and wear. It had a dozen mismatched, darker spots on it, the smallest the size of a cigarette burn and the largest as big as a basketball. On the wall next to the rug, directly across from the phonograph, was a dimestore metal-and-glass shelf that held a collection of cheap wooden jewelry boxes. The boxes were empty but open, the thin wood polished to a shine on most of them. They sat like so many gaping mouths.

Jjaks Clayton, eight years old, had sat in a beat-up chair across from the phonograph, watching his mother rock slowly back and forth to the music. She'd hum along softly with the melody, a faraway half-closed look in her eyes, her bleached blond hair swept tightly across her forehead, draped in a Marilyn Monroe bob and held in place by molasses-thick hair spray and clear bobby pins.

She would sit there until the record ended and then open her eyes as if she was waking up from sleep, and with halting movements, she'd sweep the needle back to the beginning. His mother had a photo in her hand. Jjaks had seen it often enough that he didn't have to look at it. The picture was ten years old, scratched and faded, an old publicity shot of her when she used to work the chorus lines in Las Vegas, Nevada. She worked out of The Sands for a few years, doing Broadway reviews with forty-nine other girls who had nice bodies and could kick their heels five feet in the air. Later she moved down the strip, away from the big casinos, to work for line wages and tips, waiting tables and dancing topless for fifteen minutes out of every hour. By the time she was thirty, she was too old for it. Her tits hung low enough that guys'd raise hell if they paid the cover charge and she came out and took her clothes off. Her legs cramped if she tried to dance for more than a minute or so and her lungs took to giving out on her from all the whiskey she'd drunk and from smoking two packs of Winstons a day. There were a lot of younger women, most of them snotty little bitches, just one step behind her. They reminded her of herself a few years earlier, eager to take the world by the balls, with attitudes that matched the pace of Vegas. They could move on the stage like nymphs on strong, steel-spring legs and owned tits that defied gravity.

She tended to carry the photo with her wherever she went and, oftentimes, would tell whoever was around what a big star she'd been. Jjaks was eight years old, but even he knew his mother hadn't been a star. As far as he could figure out, she was good at not wearing a lot of clothes, kicking her legs up over her head, and spending time with men who were in Vegas on business. She'd talk about breaks, look at Jjaks, and say, "If I only had a big break." He didn't know what that meant, but it sounded like it hurt.

It was Johnny Cash singing on the phono. Jjaks' mom said it was all right to know how to dance to stage tunes, but that it wasn't real music. She called Johnny Cash her "solitary-one-and-only" and told Jjaks that the man had been to prison. Jjaks wondered, was it because of his voice, the scratchy sound? They throw him in jail because of that? Or, did he learn to sing that way inside of jail? He couldn't picture it, going to jail, except for what he'd seen on television. He thought of it kind of like the Minneapolis Zoo that he'd been to one time. A lot of cages with bad guys. They'd go to jail, pace back and forth behind the bars, and then have to wait in chow lines to eat food that looked like it would stick to the wall if you threw it hard enough.

He didn't know how old his mother was. If he had to guess, he'd have said twenty-five or maybe seventy. She seemed old. Old and tired. Every day, after she got up, she spent more time in the bathroom, running a brush through her hair and smearing thick tan goop on her face.

She was mean in a way that left Jjaks wondering if she forgot who he was sometimes. She was meaner when she drank, which was about half the time she was awake. Jjaks had never seen anyone as thirsty as his mother. She worked in a factory a couple miles from the house they rented — her, Jjaks, and his older brother, Sam. Jjaks' mother said working in the factory was kin to working in a shithole and she'd often stop at one of several bars on her way home. She was fond of bringing strange men back to the house with her and then yelling at the two boys if they made a sound.

Jjaks would stay up at night listening to fighting sounds, the grunts and muted yells coming from his mother's bedroom. Sammy was six years older and had long ago cut a small hole through the wall of his mother's bedroom. He'd kneel there, in the room he shared with Jjaks, with his eye pressed up against the hole, and watch the activity, telling Jjaks to shut the fuck up if he said anything.

Now Jjaks got up from his chair and walked over to his mother. She was smoking, holding a cigarette limply in her hand. Staring out the dirty window while smoke curled up around her head in haloed rings and disappeared toward the ceiling.

He asked, "Momma . . . ?"

There was a glass of brown liquid on the table in front of her. The table had three good legs. The fourth was broken, balanced by a dirty cinder block. His mother reached slowly down, took the glass, and held it to her lips. He watched in fascination, saw her grimace against the taste, and then shudder. After she put the glass down, he said, again, "Momma?"

She looked at him. "I tol' you, you sit down an' wait." There was no anger there, just a monotone where she could have had some kind of feeling. He didn't want to sit down, didn't want to just wait for it, and he knew she was too tired to get up and hit him.

"How come" — he took a step toward her — "how come I got to go and Sammy don't?"

She looked at him. He could see lines on her face,

creases in the makeup, giving her a dirty look, like she'd been playing over on the baseball field in Landly, running the base paths, which Jjaks sometimes did. He'd go on out and pretend he was Brooks Robinson, or Willie Mays, stealing second base or driving in a run in the World Series. It was fun, but he'd catch hell when he came home with the red-color base-path dirt in his clothes. His mother would yell at him. "How the hell you think I'm gonna get that shit out, you come in here with that dirt on you?" She hardly ever washed his clothes, though; it had crossed his mind one day, sitting with her when she'd been in a good mood, watching television and seeing a commercial. Some blond woman with a big smile on her face talking about *whiter whites*. He wanted to tell his mom. See, you could try that. But then he saw she wasn't paying attention.

She leaned forward, staring out the window again in a way that made Jjaks realize he didn't have much time. There was a noise from the other end of the room and Jjaks turned to see his brother, Sammy, grinning at him from the kitchen. Sammy made a movement with his hands, a motion saying he wanted Jjaks to follow him, but Jjaks turned back to his mother.

"How come . . ." It was all he got out. She came back to life all of a sudden, sitting up in her chair and yelling at him from six inches away. "I already tol' you all I got to say. You goin' because he wants you and I can't afford two growin' boys anyhow." Behind him he could hear his brother start to giggle and he felt the hot shame of a blush on his cheeks. His mother said, "Your daddy's a sumbitch, but he'll feed you." She went back to looking out the window and said, almost to herself, "Maybe I love you, but he says he wants you, and goddamn, he's welcome to you."

Sammy made a sound from the kitchen. When Jjaks turned, his brother motioned the same as before. Jjaks waited, hoping he'd hear his mother change her mind.

When she continued to look out the window, he finally walked over to his brother.

Sammy said, "I want to show you somethin'."

"What?"

"In here."

He started into the kitchen and Jjaks asked it again, "What?"

Sam turned to him with a look of disgust on his face. "In here. I ain't gonna tell you out there. I got somethin' . . . I want you to see somethin'. You want to find out what, you got to follow me, do what I tell you."

In the kitchen, Sam turned on the stove and held his hand over the burner. After a minute Jjaks could feel the heat coming off and he took a step back. "What are you doin'? You nuts?"

His brother smiled, touching his hand to the burner fast enough that Jjaks wasn't sure he'd seen it at first. Sammy did it again. His arm was like a snake striking, snapping out, touching the burner for an instant, and then retreating just as quickly.

Sam said, "You do it."

"Uh-un."

"Chicken."

"I ain't chicken, I'm just not gonna do it." The kitchen was tiny, with peeling linoleum floors and grease stains all up the walls. There was a small refrigerator that barely worked and made so much noise that it often kept Jjaks awake at night. The only door was the one Jjaks had come through. He knew if he tried to get back out, his brother would stop him.

Sammy said, "You're chicken. Chickenshit. Little baby that Momma doesn't even want and you're too chickenshit to do it. Scared, is all." He had a grin on his face.

"I ain't scared."

"Then do it."

Jjaks pushed his own hand out, let it hover six inches

from the burner. He could feel the heat, a dry sensation that made him feel like lifting his hand farther into the air to ride the waves from the burner up to the ceiling. He moved his hand another couple of inches, until the heat was almost too much to take. Getting his nerve up to move like his brother had, ready to show Sam that there wasn't anything he could do that Jjaks couldn't do too. He was gritting his teeth, turning his arm into the same kind of snake as Sam's had been, when Sam reached out, grabbed Jjak's hand with both of his, and slammed it down on the burner.

Jjaks screamed. It felt like the burner was eating into his skin, like it was gonna saw through his bones, suck him into itself until he became a part of the stove. He didn't think he had had his hand on it that long. He wrenched his arm out of his brother's grasp almost immediately, but the pain stayed with him, destroying his flesh like it was melted butter and following him on a crazy-quilted dash around the small kitchen. He could hear his own voice, as if it came from someone else. A long, high-pitched scream. He could also hear the sound of his brother's laughter.

He finally got to the sink, spun the handle of the faucet all the way, and stuck his hand under the cold water. Behind him, Sam said, "You wanna know what that was? That was to make a mark on you. You're gonna carry that scar around your whole life. People'll know who Momma didn't want. She got rid of Chickenshit, that's what people will know."

Behind him, Jjaks could hear the scratchy, tinfoil voice of the man from prison singing. He wished the man would stop, wished his momma would get up out of her chair and turn the phono off. Maybe, then, she'd come in and do something about the fire in the palm of his hand. Maybe she'd do something about Sam and then change her mind about making him go to his dad's.

The song ended. For a moment Jjaks thought she was coming. She'd heard him thinking, read his mind somehow, and now she was coming in to tell him she'd changed her mind. But then he heard the prison man's voice start once again, low and mournful. The song was beautiful, rich and haunting, but after a minute Jjaks stopped listening.

Ain't no one was gonna come in and make things better. Nobody was gonna stop that Johnny Cash man from singing or Jjaks from being taken out of his own house and put somewhere he didn't want to be.

Ain't no one was gonna do a damn thing.

Chapter 1

MINNESOTA 1995

IT WAS HARDER THAN hell, running in a wedding gown. Satin clinging to her thighs every time she lifted a leg to take another step. The veil flowing behind her head, catching the wind and streaming back from her head as if it was her own hair. If she'd had the time, she'd have felt ridiculous.

Her feet were killing her. Every time she touched the ground it felt as if someone stuck needles into her skin. She was running on asphalt with no shoes on. Lifting the hem of the wedding dress, bunching it in her hands and counting her steps because it had become something to concentrate on, one-two, one-two, until it became impossible to separate the numbers in her head from the feel of the asphalt against the soles of her feet.

She'd seen people jogging, running in parks or along side of the road. A lot of them were fat, out of shape. You got the feeling that the first thing they did, once they were back indoors, was turn on the central air, eat a big meal, and sit in front of the TV for a couple of hours.

She had to admit some of them looked okay. Fit. Strutting in their Spandex, the women mostly, but even the men if they were vain enough. Running their asses off so maybe they'd get laid more often. Even if she had a choice, running wasn't something she figured on ever doing again. And she wasn't worried about getting laid.

There was a car behind her. A cherry GTO that belonged to the owner of the club she danced in. He wasn't there to give her a lift, pick her up, and like a gentleman, take her back into town. She had an idea, a best-case scenario, that he was going to catch up to her and make her life hell. Or, he might just get it in his head to run her the fuck down.

Her shoes were somewhere back there, behind her. Where Red's car was. Four-inch heels that were hard to walk in and impossible to run in. She'd heard the car stop earlier; the tires screeched and a door slammed. Maybe they'd picked up her shoes.

It occurred to her that perhaps no one had ever run this far. She was breaking some kind of record, so they could put her in that book, *Guinness World Records*, or whatever it was called. She thought it was the same people that made the beer, but wasn't positive. She wasn't wearing a watch but thought she'd been running for over two hours. It sure as hell felt that way. Her breath sounded to her own ears like some big train wheezing painfully up a hill.

When she'd been a kid in grade school, the entire fourth grade had gone to the Science Museum of Minnesota. One of the things they had there was a huge, old locomotive. She remembered like it was the other day. They'd fire up its engine once an hour to move it back and forth on a track a hundred and fifty feet long, while all the kids who'd climbed aboard screamed with joy.

She felt like that ancient locomotive. She'd been running

10

long enough that each time she gulped air into her lungs she got a knifelike pain in her side. She had no clue how much farther she could go.

Behind her, the car started up again. She could picture Red, behind the wheel with a cigar in his mouth, Ray•Bans over his eyes, and a diamond pinky ring the size of a small marble on hands with prominent knuckles. Red had all the money in the world, could have bought a Lincoln, a Caddy, but preferred muscle cars. The GTO was bright red, with a lot of chrome, and she wasn't going to outrun it. But she kept putting one foot in front of the other, one-two, one-two, just the same.

They were playing with her, Red and his goon. Cat and mouse. A couple of Minnestoa mobsters having a good time, while she had a goddamned heart attack and cut up the soles of her feet. Killing time, because there was still an hour to go before the wedding. Watching her run and making jokes.

She was on the west side of the city, Grant Industrial Park. A place that hopped during the week, ten thousand people working the factories and the shipping plants farther out, but was deserted on Sundays. She was running across a huge parking lot built north to south outside of a paper mill that was closed for the weekend, or closed forever. You could never tell in this town. The building was red brick on the first floor and dirty gray stucco, with a lot of glass, on the second and third floors. Most of the windows were broken. Around the building there were shards of glass, twinkling like jewels on the pavement. If the GTO headed her in that direction, she'd cut her feet to ribbons.

Two hundred yards away was another parking lot and acres even farther down, stretching like giant asphalt football fields with no end in sight. There was nowhere that she could really run to, no place to hide. But she ran anyway.

The car passed her; she could see faces, two men peering out at her. Red hit the gas and the car shot forward, turning

11

in a lazy circle and then coming back, forcing her to change direction. She could hear laughter as the car whipped by.

She stopped running and looked around for something to throw, a rock or stick that she could pick up and hurt someone with. What she'd really like was a gun, a big-caliber pistol so she could wait calmly for the car to come by again, wait until Red and his scumbag buddy got out of the car. She could show them the pistol and say, Hey, fellas, I got an idea, why'nt you take *your* shoes off and run for a while? She might as well have been on the fucking moon, though. She didn't have a gun and there wasn't a thing to throw, except for the pebbles cutting into her feet.

She put her hands on her knees and bent over, trying to force more oxygen into her tortured lungs. Watched as the car completed another circle and swung around toward her. As it got closer she started to trot.

—*m*—

RED HIT the brakes, saying, "Jesus, this broad can run." He let the car idle, staring out the windshield. "Look at her. She's got the fucking wedding dress on, where the fuck she think she's gonna get to wearing that?" He was enjoying it, the sight of the woman running frantically. Going nowhere.

The woman changed directions again, veered away from Red's car, and started to run toward the far end of the parking lot. Red chuckled. "She's seen the glass, she knows not to go near the building. This is no dumb bitch we got here. This woman's thinking for herself. Only thing is, time for thinking is over." He gazed past her, over the top of the building. Across the way he could see Interstate 35, coming down from Lake Superior. The cars were stuck, bumper-to-bumper, and looked like toys from this far away. To the west was the Minneapolis/St. Paul International Airport, and occasionally Red would see the shadow of a big jet taking off. If they kept driving this way, taking into account that they'd more than likely run out of parking lot, or Freddie, the woman running, would drop dead, they'd end up in the Mississippi River.

Red was forty years old and looked like what he was, a small-time mobster who owned four pinball arcades spread out across a small section of the city, and a strip joint on Passaic Avenue, a dive with a neon sign of a woman in a bikini above the front door and bars on all the windows.

He ran dope, mostly pot, crack cocaine, and some bootleg Quaaludes, that he'd sell in bulk to a couple of dealers across town and in small amounts, out of his arcade, to pimply-faced high-school kids who liked to get wasted and bang his machines until their thumbs fell off. He had a numbers racket covering four city blocks and a low-level shylock setup.

Red had to pay both the mob and the local police to let him stay in business. Every once in a while he'd send one of his boys out to break somebody's fingers if they decided not to pay him the money they owed. He had no reason to be out here chasing a woman down with his GTO except he'd made a deal and knew it would be good business to keep his end of it.

He'd promised to bring the girl back to her wedding, whether she wanted to go or not. Red had told Sammy Clayton, the anxious groom, I'll make sure she's there because the girl had stolen money and Sammy was the one who'd found out. But he hadn't known the girl could run this far. He knew Sammy Clayton and could see her point. But that didn't change things.

Next to him, in the seat of the car, was Joe Weston. Red said to him, "She's like an ostrich. But, when you see an ostrich, all you think is there's those skinny legs holding up an ass covered by ugly feathers." He thought about it some more, watching Freddie, and said, "Wait, I know what she's like. A cheetah. Yeah. Them things can run seventy miles an hour and look as graceful as a ballerina."

Joe looked at him and said, "Huh?"

13

Red said, "Didn't you ever watch one of those nature shows, you know, wild animals?"

Joe asked, "What's that got to do with anything?"

Red had to shake his head, get back to driving. Joe was all right, good for busting heads and running dope, but talking to him could be a waste of breath sometimes. The man owned a couple of turtleneck shirts, some slacks, and one sport coat. He wore that coat everywhere he went and liked to play with guns.

Joe said, "I don't care, you want to tell me she looks like some kind of animal? That's okay by me. She can run all day, get all sweaty. She's still a good-looking broad."

"Yeah? You think so?" Red demanded.

Joe said, "Fucking right."

"Well, no shit. First of all, she danced in my club. That means she had to be. And, number two, you think we're out here, we drove all the way here, to get an ugly broad?"

"I guess not."

"You better fucking believe it. I don't *know* any ugly broads."

Joe said, "Look at her. Where the fuck she think she's going?"

"Fuck I know. Maybe she thinks she's gonna run all the way to California." Red was getting bored. It was hot out there. "Well, let's quit fucking around. Let's get it done."

He hit the gas and the wheels hopped as the transmission jolted into gear. Within seconds they were upon the woman. He cut the wheel, spun around in front of her, and hopped out of the car in one smooth motion. He could feel the heat on his neck and shoulders, the Minnesota summer sun beating down. It always surprised him. Got so goddamn cold in the winter, how could it get this hot in the summer?

The woman had stopped. Red could hear her breathing. Her head was down, her hands grasping her knees for support. He could see her ribs where the gown stuck to her skin with sweat and, farther up, the outline of her tits. She was a

14

knockout, he had to give her that. Sweat-streaked, dirty, and gasping for breath, but still, she managed to look like all she'd have to do was wipe her face with the back of her hand and you could put a photo of her in *Playboy* magazine.

He said her name. "Freddie. Hey, Freddie. We done fucking around? Can we get this done? You wanna get ready? We can get you back in that car and get out of this heat. I got A/C in that thing." He was being patient. Willing to talk nice for a couple more seconds.

She looked up at him. Her eyes were beautiful, dusky green, almost gray, with long lashes the same color as her hair. Blond. She was almost as tall as Red, with a body that men gladly paid money to see, small waist and hips, but enough up top that you couldn't help but stare. Red thought she was a cheap slut but didn't think it took anything away from her. He was used to sluts.

She worked her mouth and Red thought she was going to say something, maybe give up, but all she did, after a second, she spit on the ground and hissed, "Kiss my ass, Red."

He laughed. "No, see, we don't got time for that. 'Sides, I ain't too sure I'd want to till after you got cleaned up."

Joe sniggered. "I'd kiss it. Don't give a fuck what she's been doing."

"Be quiet, Joe." Red looked at his watch. "We got to be back—hell, we gotta be back in twenty minutes, Freddie. Be in time for the ceremony."

"Fuck you. I'm not going back. Not you or anyone else is going to make me. Tell that freak Sammy he can find someone else."

"It's not Sammy you have to be worried about. Sammy is a freak. You got that right. But see, you want to be worried about me. I'm the one you should be trying to please."

She took a step toward Red and tried to smile. "I got an idea. Why don't you give me a ride back into town? We get near the bus station and you can drop me off. We don't have to worry about who's going to marry who today. How would that be?"

Red glanced at Joe. "You hear that? She wants to go to the bus station. There's an idea. Where you wanna go, Freddie? We put you on a Greyhound, you can head out west. Go to Hollywood."

He turned back to Freddie. "I can't do anything, ya know? I could hit you, but I can't mark up your face 'cause it's your wedding day." He looked up at the sky, as if he was deep in thought, and then, suddenly, swung his fist into her stomach as hard as he could.

Freddie bent double, gagging. Red listened to her retch and then pulled her to her feet. He was thinking, Five minutes to get her cleaned up, she could put a little makeup on. Touch-up paint. Then they could head back to Sammy Clayton's, take Como Avenue past the zoo, miss traffic hopefully, cut through Falcon Heights, and be there in twenty minutes. He leaned down and put his face right next to hers. "You think you can make a fool out of me, can steal from me and walk away? You're lucky you have a nice ass. Otherwise . . . I don't even want to think about it. You're gonna marry that little fucker Sam and you're gonna cook and clean and suck his cock and you wanna know why?"

She was still gasping. He reached over, grabbed her chin, and pulled her face up. "Because it's the worst thing I can think to do to you, that's why."

She was swaying, her eyes rolling halfway up into her head like she was going to faint. Red said, "I killed a man once. Hit him too hard and he fucking died. It was an accident, I guess. But it's something you want to think about."

She said finally, "It's not going to do any good. Tell him . . . tell Sam . . . he thinks he's getting me to marry him. First chance I get, I'll run."

"No you won't. You made this deal and that's the way it is."

Joe had moved up so he could see Freddie better. She

16

looked over Red's shoulder and said, "You wanna come closer, asshole, get a good look?"

"Joe, get back in the car," Red ordered.

"What?"

Red turned. "Get the fuck back in the car. Stay there."

Joe looked like he was going to say something but then changed his mind. He shuffled over to the car and got in. Red could see his face through the dust on the windshield, his head pressed up against the window, peering at the girl.

Freddie waited until the car door had closed behind Joe and then started to brush at the dirt on her dress. Red stood there, watching her impassively.

"You enjoying yourself?" she wanted to know.

He shrugged.

"Yeah. You are. Lots of guys like to watch me. Pay me good money to sit at the bar and watch while I take my clothes off."

Red smiled at her. "Honey, I've seen worse. I can tell you that."

He stood up, admiring what he could glimpse through the disheveled dress, and then said, "It's better like that. Fucking Sammy, little piece of shit, he'll like it better this way."

She stared at him for a moment. "How 'bout you? You like it, you son of a bitch?"

He didn't let it bother him. They were done. She could call him names if she wanted to. He shrugged again. "Like I said, I've seen worse."

"Uh-huh. The thing is, you and I both know you never seen better, though."

Chapter
2

JJAKS CLAYTON'S ASS HURT. He'd been sitting on a bus for twenty-one hours, coming from Lewisburg, Pennsylvania, the one-stop town with a bus station and a federal penitentiary. He had a letter from his mother in his pocket, an invitation to his brother's wedding. That and his four-year-out-of-date clothes, a grocery bag, and fifty dollars in his pocket. Everyone on the bus knew he was coming out of jail, waiting by himself at the bus stop. There was no other reason to be there. When he got on the bus, nobody met his eyes.

He was thirty-one years old. Traveling halfway across the country because his mother had invited him and he thought perhaps it was his last chance to reach some kind of understanding with his brother and his mother. Become a family again.

He was six-foot-one, with dirty-brown hair that in the summer got a blond tint to it if he spent enough time in the sun. He had a washboard stomach and big, rounded shoulders from lifting weights in the prison yard and working the machine press in the shop. There was a scar on the right side of his face, a jagged line of tissue running from below his sideburn to his jawline, that he'd gotten in a barroom brawl from the broken edge of a beer bottle.

A woman once told him that he had a distant look to his eyes. They'd been in bed and she'd said, "You know what you do?"

He wasn't interested but had been polite enough to ask, "What?"

The woman told him, "You look *through* people, not at them. It's like you only see what you want to see."

At the time he'd been concentrating on getting laid. He'd looked right at her, reached out, grabbed her right tit, and asked, "How am I doing now? You think I see you okay or should I put some glasses on?"

A couple of times in his life, he'd gotten dressed up. Went to a funeral once, put on a coat and tie, but felt funny about it. Ended up losing the tie and getting smashed on Irish whiskey at the wake. To his last court date he'd worn a three-piece suit, thin pinstripes on gray material. Made him look like a stockbroker. His prick of a lawyer, a public defender with a high squeaky voice who didn't like to shake hands, had lent it to him. Told him, "You got to try to impress the judge." Jjaks thought that maybe the lawyer ought to have tried a little harder in law school.

He'd put the suit on and gone before the judge. The man had listened to the evidence and then banged his gavel down. Told Jjaks he was gonna be a guest of the federal government for the next several years at least. As the marshal came up to lead him away, the only thing his lawyer had to say to him was, "Make sure I get that suit back. Don't get any dirt on it."

It didn't bother him now that he was breaking parole, leaving the state, when what he should've been doing was going to Pittsburgh or somewhere else nearby, getting a job and reporting to his parole officer first thing Monday morning. He had an idea, if he did that, the first thing that would happen was he'd go back to doing street shit, ripping people off. In a couple of months he'd be back inside the walls of that fucking penitentiary.

Instead, he'd go across country. Go to his brother's wedding, even though they hadn't spoken more than a few words to each other in years. Go back to his roots for the first time in a long time and see what happened. He was going home. He'd spent four years in prison, watching his back, trying to stay one step ahead of eleven hundred and eighty-two other convicts, some of whom were certifiably crazy and would hurt you just to make the day go faster. Before that, he'd wandered around the country working odd jobs when he got the chance. Stealing cars and holding up liquor stores when he felt lucky.

What he had in mind now was to go straight. It sounded corny as hell, you say it like that. A line from a bad movie. But it was a hard-earned fact that Jjaks had learned. Most crime, sooner or later, whether it seemed to pay or not, certainly caught up to you and gave a fellow some extra time to sit and think.

———

OUTSIDE OF Cleveland, two black guys got on the bus. They looked like any one of a dozen inmates Jjaks had spent the last four years with.

Jjaks was sitting near the back, killing time by trying to toss an unlit cigarette into his mouth. He wanted to be able to impress somebody, anybody, when he got to Minnesota. He kept hitting himself on the side of the face, but he figured he'd get it sooner or later. He was by the bathroom at the end of the bus because there was more room there.

The black dudes got on and started staring at him right away. It was dark, two o'clock in the morning. Most people

20

were asleep, letting the guy behind the wheel do the driving for them like in the commercial.

Jjaks had an idea that the black guys were giving it some thought, waiting for the next stop to be coming up and then would go back and fuck with him, take what little money he had and be off the bus before anybody knew what happened. He decided maybe they'd mistaken him for someone else.

He got out of his seat and walked up the aisle to where they sat. He could've let it go, sat back and seen whether or not he was wrong about their intentions. The thing was, though, you spend four years in a federal penitentiary and you learn not to let people look at you like that.

They watched him come, giving him their rap stares, hard-assed kids who didn't know what it was like to survive for five minutes in a federal institute of corrections.

Jjaks walked up to them, sat down on the arm of the seat across the aisle, and said softly, "See, I'm back there, I'm minding my own fucking business. I see you guys looking at me and all of a sudden I remember where I've seen you before."

The bigger guy said, "The fuck you talking, man?"

Jjaks ignored him. "Back where I was, I remember now, you were the two, when I used to want a piece of ass, get out of my cell and stick my dick in somebody's mouth, it was you two. I'd walk down D block and you two assholes would be waiting to suck me off." Jjaks had a small smile on his face that had nothing to do with being friendly. He said, "And now you're looking at me, thinking here's a white boy you can fuck up. I think maybe you boys got on the wrong motherfucking bus."

He watched something change in the bigger guy's face. A realization. The man was thinking, Uh-oh. A little less sure of himself. Used to folks caving in when he gave them his stare. Jjaks was tired and wanted to go back and fall asleep, but he had to wait for this thing to get decided.

21

Finally, the other guy said, "No man, you was wrong. We was looking out the *back* of the bus, was all."

Jjaks nodded. "Yeah, I was, I guess. I thought you were looking at me. I guess not."

"No. The *back*, man, we was looking out the back."

Jjaks went back to his seat. The thing to do here was pretend it had never happened. Let the guys chill, get over their embarrassment so they could tell themselves they hadn't meant anything anyway. Convince themselves that it wasn't Jjaks that had put a stop to their plans.

He leaned his head against the window, watching the backs of their heads through the space between the seats in front of him. At the next stop they got off, without looking at him once. He closed his eyes and went to sleep.

⸻

THINGS WERE different enough, had changed more than he thought, so that when he got to Minneapolis he had to think about which way to go to get to his mother's house.

The town seemed washed-out, as if the sun never quite got all the way above the horizon. It was sticky hot, with the air close all around. He had sweat under his shirt before he'd walked fifty feet.

Things seemed to have speeded up, in a way that he wasn't prepared for. A car would go by and Jjaks would think it was flying, going fifty miles over the speed limit. Then he'd remember that it had been four years since he'd walked along a street. He found himself, in the first five minutes, crossing the street twice because he saw people walking toward him and wondered how long was that gonna keep up? Walking along, telling himself, Man, you got to get a little control here, you got to blend.

He only had fifty dollars in his pocket but decided, fuck it. First day home, he could take a cab. The cabbie wanted to talk. He looked like he came from Iran and had a wicked accent but kept yapping all the same. He talked about the

22

weather, the city, other drivers, politics, and all kinds of shit, but Jjaks didn't pay any attention. He looked out the window at the closed businesses and boarded-up homes and thought he might've made a mistake coming here. The thing was, where the hell else could he go?

When he got to his mother's street he paid the driver and leaned in to get his bag. The cabbie said, "Hey, man, you have a nice day, huh?" He looked like he was waiting for Jjaks to give him a tip, staring right at Jjaks' face with a shit-eating grin on his face.

Jjaks said, "You talk too much, anybody ever tell you that?"

The shit-eating grin turned to a scowl. "Hey, fuck you, man." He hit the gas and the cab shot forward. Jjaks was left standing down the block from his mother's house, a beat-up grocery bag holding his few possessions, trying to decide, he was almost home, should he walk down the street or not?

~~~

LIEUTENANT BEN Costikyan knew the man was an ex-con before the cab even pulled away. The guy getting out of the taxi had a look about him, guarded, like he wasn't going to make a move until he was completely aware of his surroundings. The lieutenant had seen it a thousand times before. Prison yard, bad-assed, watch-your-back cool.

Costikyan was standing in front of Sammy Clayton's house, waiting for the bride to show. He was a big man, with beefy, chapped hands, close-cropped brownish-gray hair, a sizable gut from the shitty food he ate on the job, and a red face from too much whiskey. He wore a hat with a feather in the brim. It didn't matter what the weather was, he wore that hat every day of his life. In a holster tucked under his armpit was a Ruger .357. He kept a pint flask in there too, in the pocket opposite his holster and gun. Filled it with whiskey every morning, like breakfast, and spent the rest of

23

the day sipping from it when not too many people were looking.

He'd spent enough time practicing, thought it was important enough, that he could have that Ruger out and ready to fire in about one-point-three seconds. He lived in a two-story twin about a half a mile east of the Minneapolis/St. Paul International Airport with a woman he'd been married to for twenty-five years but tried hard never to set eyes on or talk to anymore. His wife was about as fat as anyone he'd ever met. She was five-feet one-inch tall but had to turn sideways and pay attention when she went through a doorway. She seemed to spend most of her time talking on the phone or putting food in her mouth. Costikyan sometimes forgot what her first name was. The last time he'd had sex with her was in October of 1978. He'd been drunk on tequila, and it was a thing he looked back on with regret.

He could go out in his backyard and see nothing but flat marshland and the edge of the Fort Snelling National Cemetery between his house and the closest runway. He'd set up empty bottles of Miller Beer and Jack Daniel's whiskey on a log he'd rolled sideways between him and the marsh and bang away with the .357. He considered it part of the job to be able to get a shot off quickly.

He'd shot four people, three while he was on the job and one goof who'd made the mistake of entering his house late one night without knowing whose name was on the mortgage papers. It was a junkie looking for a quick score, and Costikyan let him get all the way in and then shot him six times. All six bullets entered the junkie's chest in a circle small enough to cover with a man's hand. Costikyan enjoyed that one.

The lieutenant thought of himself as the kind of cop who worked closely with his community. He'd take a bribe from anyone. He took money from the local bookies and drug pushers to look the other way. He made sure that the hookers who were run by pimps that paid him stayed out of jail and that the freelancers gave him a blow job whenever he felt like it. He didn't make a lot of arrests because he considered it more effective law enforcement to drag some perp behind a building and beat the shit out of him. Not a whole lot of people would come to his funeral when he finally kicked but he didn't give a shit.

Behind him, he could hear the sounds of a lousy rock-and-roll band butchering a Rolling Stones song. Sammy Clayton had hired a band to play at his own wedding for a hundred bucks, spending cash like it was the middle of the Depression. Costikyan couldn't tell, were they tuning up or was that really a song?

The Claytons' house was at the far end of a narrow road where all the houses were identical. They'd been built to help house the baby boomers, and the builder had thought turning a few of them sideways would fool somebody. There were trees, maples and oaks every twenty feet or so, and most yards looked like the grass could use cutting. From somewhere, a block or so over, came the high-pitched scream of a tree chipper. There were dozens of cars lining the street. Costikyan's own car, an unmarked squad vehicle, was double-parked a few feet away. Inside the car was his new partner, Lloyd Gold, sitting in the heat.

Lloyd had gotten his detective shield a month before and they'd put him with Costikyan because they didn't know what else to do with him. Costikyan thought Lloyd was a self-righteous prick who was too dumb to even put the air conditioner on. He could sit there all day and sweat. Ben didn't give a shit about that either.

He turned his gaze back to where the wedding was going to take place. The house was a shithole. It needed to be painted, needed a new roof, and Sammy's mother, Nora, had taken to throwing bags of trash out the side door, too drunk, or lazy, to walk them out to the street where they'd be collected. You could smell them from here. Out back, he could see a few people milling around. He'd been there

25

already, killing time while he waited for Red to bring the girl, Freddie, back. Thirty people getting drunk at eleven A.M. Scum friends of Sammy and Red, not there for the wedding but to take advantage of the free booze and stale sandwiches Nora had gotten from the deli down the street. The lieutenant had the idea that everyone in the backyard had been arrested for something at some point in their lives.

Sammy Clayton was wearing a powder-blue tuxedo and pacing nervously back and forth. He was a pale, pudgy man in his thirties, slightly bowlegged, who ducked his head when he talked to you, looked off to the side more often than not. He was going bald on the top of his head and had the general air about him of a man who worried a lot about things of little consequence. He was the type who would speak up at a high-stakes poker game to ask whether it was true that three of a kind beat a pair of deuces and then not understand when somebody shot him for the general good.

Right now, in the blue tux, the man looked like some kind of overblown, pastel penguin dying of radiation poisoning. Sickly in a way a plant would be if it never got any sunlight. Sammy Clayton spent too much time eating and too much time in dark tittie bars. There was a soft, whiny quality about Sammy that made Costikyan wanna puke if he spent much time with the man.

Costikyan had watched him for a while and then gone over and said sarcastically, "Nice fucking tux, Sammy."

Sammy didn't get it. He'd looked down at the clothes. "Really? You think so? It's not too small, huh?" Sammy looked like he was gonna burst out of the cummerbund any second and his sleeves were two inches shy of his wrist.

The lieutenant looked at him and shook his head. "Jesus, Clayton, you're a fucking trip, you know that?"

Sammy had gone off to find his mother; maybe he was gonna ask her what she thought of his tux. His mother, Nora, was a piece of work too. She smelled of booze, no matter what time of day it was, and was busy running around telling all the guests that she used to be a Las Vegas showgirl. She had peroxide-blond hair, a wig that Dolly Parton wouldn't be caught dead in, and was wearing a low-cut dress and high heels that made her look like an aging streetwalker. She had prominent, purplish veins in her legs and her tits were falling out of her dress. Costikyan had the idea she'd stuffed something in there—toilet paper, whatever—to make her cleavage bigger. But he didn't care. Looking at her made his stomach sour, so he didn't spend a lot of time wondering about it.

When he turned back to the street the man who'd gotten out of the cab was standing motionless, gazing his way. It crossed the lieutenant's mind that what he could do was go on down the street and ask the guy what the fuck did he think he was doing. Except there was something vaguely familiar about him, not like the lieutenant had seen him before but as if he looked like someone else. Costikyan thought maybe he'd give it a few minutes, see what the guy decided to do.

He heard a car turn the corner, wheels screaming. The vehicle pulled up behind him and he took his time, played it cool, turning slowly and watching as Red got out of the car, followed by Joe and the broad. Jesus, looking at her, he felt something in his gut, a feeling he'd get if he swallowed a double shot of bourbon and waited while it burned a hole in his stomach.

She was dressed in the wedding outfit Sammy had picked out. Her hair was messed up, blown back by the wind and tangled in the veil, but it didn't take anything away. It gave her a wild look, the blond strands framing her face, accenting her eyes. He could imagine what it'd be like to fuck her, get that body out of the wedding dress and tear into it. Mess her hair up some more. Make her yell.

She saw him staring and made a face. He smiled, walked

27

over, and announced, when he got to the the three of them, "The blushing bride."

"Fuck you, Lieutenant."

Ben grinned even more. "Anytime, hon. You wanna get this over with, marry Sammy the fucking sleazeball. Later on today, you get bored, give me a call. We'll have ourselves a good time."

He looked at Red. "She give you any trouble?"

Red said, "Nothing I need to tell you about. We reached an understanding." Red turned to Joe. "Go get it." Had to say it again before the man walked back to the car and came back with a fat envelope. Red took it and handed it to Ben. "You gonna count it?"

"Why, should I?"

Red shrugged. "You can count it, if you want. Ain't gonna make any difference. It's all there."

Ben stuck the envelope in his jacket pocket and looked at Freddie. "See that, sweetheart. Red here, he's paying good money for you. You should be flattered."

"Gimme a break, Lieutenant. You assholes want to play your games, go ahead. First chance I get, I'm out of here."

Ben wasn't smiling. He had a hard look on his face that hadn't been there before. He reached out and grabbed Freddie's arm, pulled her to him and, at the same time, ran his other hand up her skirt and squeezed her thigh, hard. She gasped in pain and he said, "No. See, honey, you ain't gonna run. You're gonna stay right here. Make Sammy a nice little wife, and if I want, I'm gonna call you up whenever I fucking feel like it and you're going to come over and make me happy. We understand each other?"

Red said, "Yeah, I think she gets it."

"Red, I'm talking to her. You hear me ask you anything?" He turned to where Red and Joe stood, giving them a look of total contempt. "I'll tell you what, why don't you two go on back? See how Sammy's doing. Maybe he needs help

28

zipping up his fucking blue trousers. Freddie and I will have a little chat."

He thought Red was going to say something, put up a fuss. But all he did, after a long moment, he shrugged and said, "Hey, you two wanna talk, it's okay by me."

Chapter 3

RED TOOK THREE STEPS away from Freddie and the lieutenant but had to turn around and say to Joe, "Whatta you doing? You gonna stand there for the next month? Jesus," because Joe was looking from Ben to Sammy to Red with an expression of disbelief on his face. Red stood there until Joe got it through his head that they were supposed to walk away and leave Ben alone with the woman.

When Joe caught up to him the first thing he said, was "How come you let him do that?"

Red told him to shut the fuck up and then walked him up to the front porch of the house. They stood there, under the sagging awning, and watched while the lieutenant stuck his face close to Freddie's and talked to her.

Red said, "See that, Costikyan's sweet on her."

Joe said, "He's what?"

"You heard me, he's sweet on her. It's different than wanting to get laid, wanting to get your cock sucked. You want that, what difference does it make who does the sucking?

Hell, she ain't even got to be good-looking, if you turn the lights down low enough."

"So?"

"So, every once in a while a woman'll come along and do something to a man's head. That's what's happening down there."

After a while Red asked, "Joe, you see them out there, what do you think you're looking at, a high-school kid and his fucking prom date?"

"Red, I'm not talking about that. The prick wants to talk to the girl, I can't blame him. I'd wanna talk to her too."

"Yeah? You wanna talk to the girl? Why is that? 'Cause she's got a nice ass and a great set of tits. You got the same thing on your mind that Costikyan does: pussy." He nodded his head in the direction of the couple. "Look at him." He laughed. "Christ, look at him."

Red had decided he'd go over and bust up the lieutenant's party. Tell him enough was enough. But Sammy came hurrying up to him.

Red put a smile on his face. It took a little effort, seeing Sammy all anxious and acting like he was about to piss his pants. Sammy was turning from Red to where Freddie and Costikyan were huddled and Red had to snap his fingers in the man's face to get him to quit moving so much.

Red said, "Well, there she is. Your Christmas bonus. A few months early, is all."

"God. She's beautiful."

Red said, "Yeah, I got to admit that much. She is one fine woman."

"What's she doing over there? That's a cop—Lieutenant Costikyan, right?"

"Yeah, sure. Don't worry about it. I think, what it is, the lieutenant knows some people, mutual friends, you know. They're saying hello." Costikyan had his hand on Freddie's shoulder now, half patting and half stroking her back. As

31

they watched he let his hand slide down to her breast. Sammy said, "Hey . . ."

Red said, "Listen, Sammy, I'm gonna give you a piece of advice. The lieutenant, he'll be finished talking to her any minute, and until then, whyn't you just wait here. You're not even supposed to see the bride until the ceremony."

Joe spoke up from behind. "Yeah, so don't worry, if the lieutenant's copping a feel. It ain't like he's the first."

"Don't say that shit."

Red grabbed Sammy by his tux. At first his grip was strong, as if he was about to rip Sammy's jacket off, but then he relaxed. He brushed at Sammy's shoulders like the man had dandruff. "Sammy, you got to know one thing. This girl, Freddie, I don't know what you're expecting. But shit, boy, I had her. Half of Minneapolis had her. So don't make any big deal if she's talking to a cop. Any minute now she's gonna be your wife. Okay?"

Sammy looked like he was about to cry, his face all scrunched up in a peculiar manner, as if he'd smelled something and was trying to decide whether or not it was edible. He had a slight overbite, and Red had noticed that when he got nervous he tended to suck in his lower lip. Made him look like some kind of giant rodent. He was like that now, with his chin up a little. Red had the idea that if he ran down to the store and got a Magic Marker, he could paint whiskers on Sammy's face and everybody would take it in stride. Start throwing big pieces of cheddar cheese at him.

"You get my drift?" Red asked.

"Is she all right?" Sammy asked back. "I mean, she ain't getting arrested or anything?"

"She's fine. A little nervous is all."

"And she's all mine."

Red nodded. "She will be in a little while. She's gonna be your wife."

Sammy almost sighed. He looked up at Red. "I just want to thank you, you know. . . ."

"I'll tell you something, you break down and cry, make a fool of yourself, and I'll get pissed off. Call this whole show off. You hear me?" He thought it was pathetic the way Sammy acted. He stared hard at him until Sammy nodded.

"Yeah . . . I understand."

" 'Cause all you're doing, you're marrying some dumb bitch. That's all. Ain't no big thing." He looked at the sky. There were clouds coming in from the west, high up and dirty looking. It was all he needed, a fucking thunderstorm. Cap off a day he wished had never begun.

It had all started because Sammy kept Red's books and he'd figured ways to save Red a lot of money. Could make it look like Red's legitimate businesses didn't make any money and could also hide the money Red made from sharking and taking bets. While Red was running shit crack cocaine and pot into the meaner streets, Sammy could hide it in the supposed losses of Red's four pinball arcades. Sammy had found where Freddie had been taking money.

Red had made the mistake of asking Sammy if he, Red, could do anything for him and Sammy said he wanted a wife. Went to Red's club with him and pointed out Freddie. Sammy had said, "Lemme ask you something."

"Sure."

"What do you think of her?"

"Who, the broad dancing? Freddie? I think she stole money from me and she's in a world of trouble."

"Uh-huh. But what do you *think* of her?"

"What do I think? I think you're talking about one of the better pieces of ass in town."

"She's good-looking."

"Hell, boy, good-looking is something you say about your cousin, if you're being nice. This girl ain't good-looking. With those tits? She looks like a centerfold come to life."

"Well, I want to marry her," Sammy had declared.

"That's what I want." He had his chin stuck out, stubborn, like a little kid who knows what he wants for Christmas.

Red thought he was kidding at first. He stood up and stared at Sammy.

"You're fucking with me, huh?"

"No."

Red thought it was crazy to want some cheap slut who took her clothes off so much that it'd save a lot of time if they were held on with Velcro. But, he figured, it was easier to give away Freddie than to kill Sammy. Sammy was too valuable to whack anyway, long as he kept doing his work.

So here they were, stuck in a shitty backyard with trash bags heaped up along side of the house and a smell like maybe the sewer was going to overflow, or somebody in the neighborhood had a pet hog.

Sammy was about to marry the dancer. He'd seen her tits a couple of times in a bar and fell in love with them. Red agreed to it finally, because it was the only thing that would make Sammy happy. And Sammy knew too much to be un-happy.

—m—

LIEUTENANT COSTIKYAN waited until he knew Red and Joe were out of earshot. Then he turned back to Freddie. "Now, how we doing?" he asked.

She had a nervous look on her face. Almost scared. But hard too. He liked that. There were two kinds of people that Costikyan knew of. Survivors. And those that they ate.

He took a long look at Freddie. Maybe she didn't look like a fashion model, but that was because of the dirt on the dress she had on and the dirt on her feet. But if you looked past that, you saw something else. Costikyan did, at least. He saw a survivor.

He could tell she wanted to remain silent, didn't want to give him the satisfaction of answering. He squeezed her thigh harder. "You already got a couple of bruises on you.

34

You want me to tear your leg off? You can hop down the fucking aisle, for all I care."

There were tears in her eyes now. She said, softly, "Please . . ."

He let go of her, pulled his hand away from her thigh, and dragged it slowly upward, across her crotch. "There you are. It's easy. Ain't no one saying you got to love Sammy. All you got to do is marry the motherfucker for now. Understand?"

"Shit, what do you care? You don't even like Sammy Clayton."

"The man's a piece of shit. I admit that. But what I want is, I want to be able to know where you are. You go running around town by yourself, what happens if I want to look you up, spend some time with you? I got to hunt all over the place." He turned her so she was looking up at Sammy's house. "This way, you live here, make Sammy a happy little fucker, and I'll know where you are all the time."

"You're a pig."

"No, I'm not a pig. I'll tell you what I am, though. I'm a married man with a fat ugly wife who'll take me for every cent I have if I try to leave. I see a young thing like you, hey, it's a two-way street. You make me happy and I'll do all right by you."

"Shit."

He grinned. "Uh-un, no shit." He turned to head for his car. The man that had gotten out of the cab was still standing there. As the lieutenant reached his car the man started to move, walking slowly toward Sammy Clayton's house.

Costikyan paused, seeing it again, something familiar about the man's face. He memorized it, storing it in his head where he put all the faces of scum he might run into again. He watched the man for another few seconds and then climbed into his car.

His partner, Lloyd Gold, was sweating. Ben started the car, turned the air conditioner on full blast, and looked at

Lloyd. "You know, they got this thing in here, A/C, it gets rid of the heat."

Lloyd said, "It's not good for the car to let it sit and idle with the air conditioner on."

"Not good for it, huh?"

"The car will overheat."

The lieutenant put the car in gear. "You worried about overheating the car. This your car, Lloyd? Or is it a piece of shit that belongs to the city?" He pulled down the street, past the man walking toward the wedding party, and said to Lloyd, "You know, you're a fucking dickweed, Lloyd. I don't know, were you born that way or did you have to practice? But you . . . you are a fucking dickweed. Anybody ever tell you that?"

RED HEARD Costikyan's car take off. He took Freddie by the arm and walked her around the house. He knew Sammy was following. Sammy was like a puppy dog who'd wet the floor, cowed, with his tail between his legs. Red had the feeling he could put Freddie at the bottom of a cliff, show Sammy where she was, and tell him, She's all yours. Then he'd stand back while Sammy jumped and held his nose.

He was squeezing Freddie's arm hard, leaning down to talk to her as they made their way past the trash. "You see what happened back there. Not only do I got to chase you all over the place, but I got to pay the lieutenant a fucking bundle of money so he lets me do this. In other words, I'm like a loan shark, gave a lot of money for you. Now you better not fuck me over."

"Red, I didn't ask for this."

"It doesn't matter. You're what Sammy wants. Asshole thinks he's getting the Virgin Mary." Red laughed. "You want me to let you go? I'll get my money back from Costikyan and he'll throw your ass in jail. Don't think he won't."

"What for? I didn't do anything. You think I'm the only girl to ever take her clothes off and dance topless in a bar?"

"Shit, woman, listen to me. You don't have to be doing anything wrong. He'd still lock your ass up. He'll make shit up about you. You better believe he will." He glanced back at the front of the house before continuing. "You got to un-derstand—Costikyan, he's a crazy motherfucker. Doesn't care about anything 'cept what he wants right here and now. I'm telling you this for your own good. He doesn't care what happens. The thing is, once he makes a deal, he'll get pissed off if somebody tries to back out. It'd be an insult."

There were two tables set up and about a dozen different kinds of chairs set in misaligned rows. Somebody had taken a lawn mower and cut a six- or seven-foot long swatch through the grass. The rest was about eight inches high. Looked as if someone had cleared just enough room for an aisle and then said, Fuck it.

On one table there were maybe a dozen liquor bottles. About that many people were standing around drinking. There were sandwiches, little triangular-shaped things on stale-looking bread with wilted lettuce, on another table. A lot of flies there, but no people.

Still holding Freddie's arm, Red marched past the other guests in the backyard, moving toward a fat, middle-aged woman who appeared to be drunk and was standing alone.

He stopped six feet in front of the woman and let go of Freddie's arm. He thought for a minute that she might run, have another try at the hundred-yard dash. But all she did was rub her biceps and then glance at him. Her eyes then traveled the circle and came to rest on the house. He saw her take it in, see what a dump it was, and then she said softly, "Shit."

"Get used to it. Nobody's fooling around here. I owe Sammy a favor and he's dumb enough to want it to be you. You fuck this up and you're gonna piss me off. Piss the lieu-tenant off. We clear on that?"

Sammy hustled up to them as Freddie was nodding to Red. The man had an expression on his face like he'd been playing with his genitals, half-excited and half-unsure of himself. He looked at where Freddie was rubbing her arm. Red thought he was going to say something, but all he did was get a silly-assed grin on his face.

He said, "We're all set." Acting happy. Red wondered, did Sammy believe that Freddie wanted this? Was he fooling himself or was he putting on a act? Ever since Sammy had set eyes on Freddie, he'd acted like she was some kind of prom queen. The man was lovestruck. Like a dog in heat that couldn't see the car coming down the middle of the street.

Red pushed Freddie from behind, moving her closer to the fat woman. "Freddie, Honey, say hello to your mother-in-law," he told her.

Sammy said, "Red, I thought . . . I thought I'd make the introductions. You know, introduce my new wife to my mother."

"What . . . ?"

Sammy squirmed. "Well . . . I guess it's not important."

"Look, you got a wedding here. Like I promised. Just 'cause you're getting married, don't let it go to your head."

"I didn't mean it like it sounded, Red."

"Yeah?"

But Sammy wasn't listening anymore. He was looking over Red's shoulder at Freddie. Joe and another of Red's men had wandered over and were standing in front of her.

Sammy said, "Fellas . . . ?"

The men paid no attention. Freddie was facing the other direction, toward Sammy's mother, not talking to anyone. Joe reached out nonchalantly, lifted the hem of her wedding dress, and burst out laughing. Somebody else whistled.

Sammy turned to Red. "What the hell are they doing that for?" He yelled, "You want to cut that out?"

Red laughed and called out to Joe, "You hear that?

38

Sammy's a little concerned you might be paying too much attention to his new bride."

Joe held his hands up in the air. "Hell, no," he said. "I didn't mean nothin'. Alls I was doing was trying to see what kind of material it was. It wasn't like I was looking at the broad's ass."

Sammy said, "Stay away from her." His voice came out almost in a whimper.

Freddie looked at him in disgust and then turned to Joe. "You're a cheap little hood," she spat. "You ever do that to me again and I'll cut your face up." Joe took a step back. He had a murderous look on his face. He moved back toward Freddie with a clenched fist.

Red said, "That's enough." He had to say it again and Joe finally stopped.

Sammy said, "What kind of a way is that to act?"

Red looked at him like he thought Sammy might be retarded. "Listen to me, douche bag. You think this is some kind of nice girl you picked out? I told ya. I had her. We all had her. Half the people born in this state have fucked her at some point. You wanna marry her, that's all right by me, it's your goddamn fantasy. But don't think she's some kind of saint."

Sammy said, "That's not true." He was staring at Freddie and seeing something that wasn't there. Red thought maybe it was because the girl was so goddamn beautiful. Sammy couldn't see past that.

"It's not true," Sammy repeated.

Red shook his head. "Jesus, boy, where do you get your ideas?" He said to Freddie with a chuckle, "Man thinks he's marrying an angel. Can you beat that?"

In the silence that followed, Sammy's mother burped loudly. Everyone looked at her. She had a pint bottle of some kind of liquor in her hand. She took a long swig of it, stepped up to Freddie, and mumbled, "Don't be calling me Mom, you hear? You call me Nora. I can't stand to be

called Mom. Ain't that right Sammy?" She hiccuped.
"Can't stand anyone calling me Mom."

Sammy turned toward her slowly. "Yes, Mom."

SAMMY WAS telling himself it didn't matter. These guys were
kidding him, saying shit like that about Freddie and lifting
her dress. He pictured it as some kind of prewedding ritual,
even though he wasn't sure. He was one of the guys, was all.
Him and Red and Joe, it was what men did, make cracks
about the wife just before the ceremony. He didn't like it,
Joe putting his hand on Freddie's dress, but he figured that
was part of it. He just wanted to hustle them all up to the
makeshift altar.

His mother had walked with him over to the side of the
backyard. She was weaving slightly, out of breath, and her
eyes were red-rimmed. When they were fifteen feet away
from the guests, she said to him, "I wonder if your brother
is going to show up?"

"What?"

"Jjaks. I wonder whether he'll come?"

"What do you mean, why would he come?"

"I invited him."

"*Jjaks?*"

"Yes. I wrote him, told him it would be okay if he
dropped by."

"You invited him to my wedding? Without even asking
me?"

"He's your brother. I told him it wasn't right if he didn't
show up to his own brother's wedding."

"Jesus, Mom . . ."

"Sammy, are you listening to me? You and Jjaks haven't
seen each other in a long time, so if he does come, please,
try to get along."

Sammy looked back at the wedding party. He could see

Freddie clearly. Then he heard his mother's voice saying, "Sam, I'm talking to you."

"Yes. I hear you. I'll try to get along with Jjaks." He began to walk back toward Freddie, not thinking about Jjaks any longer. He thought Freddie really did look like an angel. She'd make a fine wife. Her dress was torn and she looked disheveled, dirty, but it didn't matter. Only he could see what she truly was. A beautiful girl who would be his wife.

He thought of what she'd look like without the dress, her skin pale enough that in a certain light you could see the dull blue of her veins just underneath the surface. Blond hair that shimmered even now. Looked like she'd just run shampoo and clear stream water through it. Long dancer's legs like his mother's had been, before she stopped taking care of herself.

He looked around until he found Red. The man was walking to the booze table, a path clearing for him like he was Moses at the Red Sea. Sammy went over to him and whispered, "Let's go. Can we start? Where's the minister?"

Red said, "Minister? Hell, I got the justice of the peace. Ain't no minister who'd come to this house and perform a wedding."

"Well, where is he? Let's get this over with."

"You afraid she might run again? That it, Sammy boy?"

"Don't say that. She's nervous, is all. She don't know the good deal she's getting." He seemed to hesitate and then he reached into the pocket of his rented tuxedo and pulled out a brochure. "Look at this."

Red took the brochure and studied it. "What the fuck is this?"

"It's a house, a new tract they're putting up outside of town, where the old electrical plant used to be. Right on this side of Richfield. Off Route 494. Called Sunny Acres. I bought one. For Freddie and me. Got a quarter-acre lot, get to cut my own lawn. All that shit."

"You bought one?"

"I can move in there next week."

"Where'd you get that kind of money?"

Sammy knew he'd said too much. He tried hard to get an unconcerned look on his face. "I only put down a little bit, not even twenty percent. I gotta pay mortgage insurance and everything." He realized he'd better change the subject, so he said, "Where is he, that justice guy?" and made a show of looking past Red's shoulders at the crowd.

Red turned around, spotted Joe, and called out, "Joe, go get the fucking justice, he's probably inside trying to fuck Sammy's mom or getting drunk. Tell him I ain't paying him to quench his thirst, at least not till the wedding's over."

Chapter 4

JJAKS HAD REACHED THE edge of the front yard. He put his bag in the bushes and looked up at the house. It was the same as he remembered, only more overgrown. The big oak tree in the middle of the front yard was the one he used to climb for fun and to get away from Sammy. The house seemed smaller and dingier. It didn't look like it needed to be painted because it didn't look like it had ever been painted in the first place. There were weeds everywhere in the yard and a mailbox that had fallen over and was resting in the dirt as if it had been built there on purpose.

He counted six broken windows in the time it took him to glance at the front of the house. Someone had put cardboard over some of the broken panes, giving the house a dark, deserted look.

He tried to feel something, come up with some kind of happy memory, but wasn't able to. There were two ways of looking at the house, two feelings Jjaks got while he stared at it. Jesus, what a dump, and Jesus, what a *fucking* dump.

'Course, maybe if he heard a little Johnny Cash, that'd make all the difference.

He could see people out back. He'd caught a glimpse of his brother, at least it looked sort of like Sammy. But the man he saw had put on fifteen pounds and lost some of his hair. If it was Sammy, he looked like the "before" picture of a fitness advertisement. He was wearing a tux that didn't fit too well, tight around the belly and too short in the sleeves, and made him look worse.

Sammy was talking to a beefy man with red hair who seemed to be telling him something, giving him an order. Sammy looked vaguely scared.

Jjaks stopped where he was and watched until the two of them moved out of sight. Seeing his brother like this, it unsettled his stomach. He thought he might have been crazy to come home. What in the world did he expect was going to happen? Everybody would hug each other?

He hadn't seen his mother yet. The only image he had of her was when he was young and she used to dress up in her old nightclub dancing costume from Vegas. She'd get drunk and twirl around the house with her tits practically falling out of the sequined dress. She'd make Sammy and Jjaks watch and applaud. She used to tell them, "You might not know it, but soon, any day now, that phone's gonna ring and I'll get another chorus-line job. Just you wait."

He'd seen her a couple of times over the years, but it had been a good six or seven years since the last time. Now here he was.

He saw Sam again. He was walking hurriedly with a gorgeous blond woman, following in her footsteps and having trouble keeping up. The woman looked furious. With a pleading expression on his face, Sam put a hand on her shoulder. She acted like she wasn't even aware that Sammy was there.

While Jjaks watched, the blond shrugged off Sammy's hand. Sammy, pissed, stalked away. The woman turned,

44

heading in Jjaks' direction, saw him, and got a surprised look on her face.

It was just the two of them. Jjaks couldn't believe what he was seeing. It didn't make sense, a woman this beautiful hanging around Sammy.

He stood there, nervous all of a sudden, because what the hell was she doing there and what could he say to her? She was wearing a wedding gown . . . Jesus, was she the woman Sammy was going to marry? It came down to the middle of her thighs. Jjaks wondered, had designers gone to some kind of ragged style while he was in prison, it was chic to get married wearing clothes that looked like a dog had chewed on the material?

It didn't matter, though. She was gorgeous. She had high cheekbones and beautiful, haunting eyes, hair the color of the sun on a bright spring day, and long legs. There were a couple of twigs stuck in the material of her dress and a smear of grease across the calf of her left leg. There wasn't a place on her body that the dress didn't touch, it was that tight. Jjaks had trouble bringing his gaze back up from her legs.

She crossed her arms over her chest and regarded him with an amused look, as if she could read every thought in his head.

When she moved her hand to swipe at an insect, he saw she had an amateur-looking tattoo inked into her flesh just below her shoulder. The word *slut* was easy to read. He wondered, what had possessed her to have that put there? She must have seen where he was looking, because when he glanced up she was busy covering it up again with her free hand.

He couldn't take his eyes off her. It wasn't even lust, he was fairly sure of that. Or maybe it was. Or something even more than lust. It was as if he was looking at the swimsuit issue of *Sports Illustrated* come to life. Looking at those women, it always seemed as if they weren't real. It was how he felt, watching this girl walk toward him.

She stopped and stood with one hand on her hip. Poised. She managed to look like a model, fully clothed, but getting ready to pose for an underwear ad that guys all over America would fantasize about.

Her voice was husky. "I don't know, there's a yard full of scumbags in the back. I haven't seen you before. You one of *them*?"

Jjaks grinned. "No."

"Well, if you were, this conversation would be over."

"You having a bad day?"

She laughed. "You could say that." She turned, gazing back at the house, and then asked, "Looking for someone?"

"Don't know yet."

She took a step toward him. "Maybe you're looking for me."

She had dirt on her knees. He couldn't understand it. She was all dressed up in a beautiful but torn outfit, looking wonderful, but also looking like maybe she had climbed a mountain before she came here. He said, "See, I could be dreaming this, it's one explanation. Maybe I haven't woken up yet this morning."

"Uh-huh." She sank to her knees. There was a flower in the grass at Jjaks' feet, a dandelion, but she reached over slowly, plucked it out of the ground, and held it to her nose.

Jjaks couldn't take his eyes off her. He realized she wasn't wearing a bra. He got a quick peek at the top of her tits and then she pinched him hard on the thigh.

"Jesus, what'd you do that for?"

"You dreaming now?"

"No."

"See?" She handed the flower to him, leaning forward. This time he could see her breasts clearly. She said, "This is for you." Then she stood up, turned away, and started to walk toward the backyard.

46

Jjaks followed her around to the rear of the house. When he got there he realized she had waited for him. There was a tub with cans of beer and ice cubes in it and he asked her, "Can I get you a beer?" He reached down, picked up two cans, and popped one for her and the other for himself.

"What's your name?" she asked.

"Jjaks."

"Jack?"

"No. Jjaks."

"Jjaks what?"

"Clayton."

She had taken a sip of her beer and now she almost spit it out. "You're related to him?"

"Sammy? Yeah, he's my brother."

"Jesus, I don't know who's worse off, you or me." She paused, staring off into space, and then said, "Me."

"That doesn't sound like a happy bride."

She pointed toward the crowd of guests. "You see those guys, Red, he's the one with the red hair, right? And the guy with him, Joe? Those two guys would ruin anyone's day."

She had put her beer can on the table and now she bent down to pick it up. He couldn't help himself, he had to look. Stared right down her dress, even though he knew she was having fun with him. Seeing her breasts and starting to feel something in his crotch. His eyes were glued and she didn't seem to care at all.

When he finally tore his eyes away, finally looked up at her face, she was grinning. She whispered, "You shy?"

He cleared his throat. "No."

"That's good. That's fine. By the way, my name's Freddie. You got a car?"

"No."

"What'd you do, walk here?"

"More or less."

"Well, if you don't have a car, you aren't going to do me much good."

47

"You going somewhere?"

She glanced back at the house. "Soon as I can. Just as soon as I can."

Jjaks could see, over her shoulder, his brother making his way toward them. Sammy walked up and said, "He ain't heavy, he's my brother." He looked Jjaks up and down. "Jesus, Jjaks, you didn't have to get all dressed up on my account." He put his arm around Freddie, but Freddie shrugged it off and stepped closer to Jjaks.

"Hey, Freddie," Sammy suddenly announced, "my brother spends a lot of his time in prison. Isn't that right, Jjaks."

Jjaks said softly, "Whenever I can get away." He walked away from the two of them.

━━━

HIS MOTHER came out of the house a minute later looking like she'd spent the morning sipping gin. She smelled like it too. She walked up to Jjaks and peered at him through half-open eyes. Eyes that opened all the way, though, after she recognized him.

She gasped. "Oh my God, you made it."

He tried to smile. His mind was still on the blond woman. Finally, he came up with, "Hey, Nora, been a long time, huh?"

She burped. "A long time. Is that all you can say? You forget how to write? Can't use a phone?"

"Mom, I was in jail. I think if anybody should have written, it could have been you."

"I did write."

"Swell, four years and all I get is a wedding invitation."

"Well, you made it at least."

"That's right, I did."

She moved closer to him. "You bring a gift?"

"A *what*?"

She stank of booze. Jjaks had to step back or he thought he'd be nauseous.

"A gift."

"Why, what the hell for?"

"For the bride and groom. For your brother."

"No, I didn't bring a gift. When would I have had time to get one?"

"You didn't?"

"How could I? I didn't even know they were getting married until I got your letter. Besides, there isn't a lot of shopping you can do where I was. So—no, Nora, I didn't get a gift. It must have slipped my mind."

"They make a nice couple."

"A couple of what?"

"Jjaks, behave yourself."

"Behave myself. Is that all you have to say?"

She turned to face him, swaying slightly. He thought for a second that she might go over, fall down. She had an expression on her face, disoriented. It reminded him of an injured animal, already been hit by one car but not quite dead, waiting in the middle of the road for the next car to come along and finish the job.

"Can I tell you something. . . ?" he began.

"I don't want to hear nothin' from you. I figured it out, remembered why it was that I sent you to live with your father and not Sammy. Sammy was a good boy."

"Sammy held my hand on the stove and burned the shit out of it. He wasn't a good boy."

"See, that's just like you. He was a child, he didn't mean it."

Jjaks remembered the look on his brother's face, happy, when he'd held his hand on the hot burner. "Your golden boy meant it, all right."

"So give it to them."

She wasn't making sense. He was having trouble keeping up with her. "Give what to them?"

49

"Your gift."

"Nora, there is no gift."

"You show up empty-handed? What's the matter with you?"

It crossed his mind to give her a push. He could shove her and enjoy watching her fall to the ground. Step over her and go find the beautiful blond again. Ask her, Why the fuck are you marrying my asshole brother?

But he didn't. Instead he shook his head slowly. "You think I should feel embarrassed, not getting a gift?"

"You should."

"Yeah?"

"You got time. Go get them something."

"Now?"

"Yeah. Go get a gift. It's a wedding. What kind of person would come to a wedding and not bring a gift?"

It was getting to him. Not really the thought that he didn't have a gift. He didn't care for Sammy enough to buy him anything. But the thought that his mother would make a big deal out of it if he stayed and didn't have something to give the wedding couple. She'd make sure everybody knew it, make it sound like he knew about the wedding and was just too cheap to get anything.

He asked, "When's the ceremony?"

"Huh?"

"The wedding. How soon?"

She looked at her wrist as if expecting to find a watch there. There wasn't one, but she squinted up at him and said, "I don't know. The justice of the peace just got here, so I guess in a half hour or so."

"Well, there's time, then, right?"

"Time for what?"

"Don't you worry about it. I'll be back."

She smiled finally and it dawned on him that she was not all there anymore. She was living in some kind of fog. "Are

50

you going to get a gift?" she was saying. "That's great, Jjaks. Sammy'll be so pleased."

He shook his head. "Sammy won't give a fuck. You and I both know it. But I don't care about that."

He was thinking he didn't want to look like a fool in front of Freddie, didn't want to seem like the cheap ex-con younger brother that no one liked. He left his mother standing in the middle of the yard and started to walk toward the street. He remembered a store, not too far away, a couple of blocks. A gift shop. It was probably open if it was still there. He had some money in his pocket. What the hell, a pawnshop would have something appropriate.

~~~

THE JUSTICE of the peace was drunk. He was a man in his sixties, with a thin white beard and white hair parted in the back and combed all the way to the front, held in place with what looked like contact cement.

Red had to tell him four times to speak the fuck up. He managed to get through the ceremony, slurring his words but getting the point across. The man was droning on and on, putting half the crowd to sleep. Sammy stepped forward finally and told the man, "You want to hurry this shit up, get to the part where I say *I do*."

The justice looked startled, like he'd been awakened unexpectedly from a nap, but then jumped ahead. Sammy heard his name, Sam Clayton, do you . . . ? and responded, "Yeah . . . yeah."

When it was Freddie's turn she hesitated long enough that people started to snicker in the audience.

Sam said, "Yeah, she does too."

The justice said, "I'm afraid the young woman will have to answer for herself."

Sammy said, "She just did."

The justice decided to take a stand. Wyatt Earp at the fucking OK Corral. He folded his arms across his chest,

51

stared back at Sammy, and asserted, "Uh-un." It made Sammy want to go into the audience, borrow a chair, and bean the motherfucker with it. He stared hard at Freddie instead. He wanted to hit her too, make her nod her head. But he was afraid that if he did strike her, she'd run again. He couldn't take that embarrassment.

Out of the corner of his eye he saw Red take a step forward, a low animal noise coming from his throat. Freddie saw it too. She took a deep breath, looked up at Sammy with contempt, and said, "Why the fuck not?"

It wasn't the most stirring ceremony, but Sammy thought it would do.

———

SAMMY HAD bought some cold duck. Went down to the liquor store and sprang for twelve bottles. Two forty-nine apiece. He popped one now, happy as a clam that it was over and Freddie was his.

He was standing with Red, Nora, Joe, and a couple of other guys. Behind them were some other people. A bartender that worked at Slim Tie's Bar and Grill, a place where Sammy ran a tab. Sammy had mentioned the wedding to him, but he didn't remember telling the guy to show up. There were a couple of women too, over by the drink table, that Sammy was pretty sure were hookers. They were either there working or they'd come with some of Red's men. There were a few stragglers in the crowd too, people that Sammy didn't even know. Maybe they didn't have anything else to do, or Red had told them to show. Sammy didn't care. He was happy.

He held the bottle up in the air, let some of it spill down his face and chest, and then took a deep drink. It tasted like fermented Kool-Aid. He swallowed and then said, "Holy shit." He held the bottle out to Freddie.

FREDDIE LOOKED at Sammy, the cold duck dripping down his chin and the stupid expression on his face, and said slowly, "Go fuck yourself, asshole." She stepped away from him, went to the table where the wedding cake was, and cut a big piece out of the center. She could see Sammy's brother, Jjaks, sitting by himself on an aluminum folding chair fifteen feet away. She wandered over, holding the cake in one hand and picking at it with her fingers. When she got to where Jjaks was sitting, she put a piece of cake in her mouth, chewed slowly, and then ran her tongue across her lips.

She said, "The ceremony bring you to tears?"

"It was very moving."

"I'll bet." She looked across the patio. Sammy and the others were still drinking cold duck. She leaned down to Jjaks, put her face close to his, and whispered, "You want to know what I'm gonna do?"

"What?" He was staring into her eyes.

"I'm gonna go to the bathroom. I'm gonna go pee. So, if anyone wanted to find me in the next minute or so, that's where I'll be."

"In the bathroom?"

"That's right. You have any idea how hard it is"—she touched the fabric of her dress—"to get this thing off and then back on? It's almost like you can't do it alone."

He reached over, picked a piece of her cake up with his finger, and then stuck his finger in his mouth. "The bathroom, huh?"

SHE SLAMMED herself against his body, tearing at the thin material of his shirt, clawing at it as if it was oxygen and she was suffocating. Jjaks couldn't believe the intensity in her eyes, the look of animal passion.

She took her hands off of him long enough to claw at her clothes. She threw her veil on the floor and pressed herself against him, forcing him back up to the sink. Behind her he could hear a knock on the door and the sound of a voice raised in puzzled frustration.

"Hey, come on, people out here got to use the 'cilities, man."

Freddie was on her knees, yanking Jjaks' shoes off, pulling at his pants leg, first one and then the other, sliding his underwear down and then running her hand up the length of his thigh and resting it in his crotch. He felt himself start to get hard, felt the warmth from her hand spread from between his legs all the way up his back.

He heard more pounding on the door and murmured through clenched teeth, "Jesus . . ."

"Shhhhh." She stood up and kissed him. She pulled the hem of her dress up so that he could see her underwear, tiny white panties that were satin smooth and seemed to move in the glare of the small fluorescent light over the sink. They had a patch of lace in the front, a small vee like the path an arrow would take on its way to a target. Jjaks hooked a finger in the vee and pulled downward. He could feel Freddie's breath start to come more quickly, short harsh gasps that seemed to fill the air.

He said, "Sammy's right outside."

"So? What are you worried about him for?"

"I'm not worried about him, I'm worried about me."

She shoved him. "Do you think now's the time to be worrying about anything?"

He pushed back, felt her move against the sink. She was bent over now, her body levered at the waist, and he could see drops from the leaky sink faucet sprinkle onto her hair. She shook her head and droplets flew out against his face.

From the other side of the door a man yelled, "What's going on in there? I got to take a leak."

Freddie said, "I'll just be a minute." She stepped away from the sink, forcing him to move with her, and said, "Not like this." Pushing him down to the bathroom floor. "Like this."

When he was on the floor she swung one leg over his body and straddled him, lowered her weight onto him so that he entered her slowly but in one long smooth motion. He felt his stomach knot up, felt liquid warmth spread like fire across his belly.

She said, "Oh God, yes. Move a little to the left . . . move a . . . little to the right. Yes . . . bulls-eye."

She moaned and grabbed his hand, lifted it to her face, and stuck one of his fingers into her mouth. Before he knew what she was going to do, she had bitten down on his finger hard enough to draw blood.

He said, "Jesus," and almost yanked his finger out of her mouth, but he was too overcome with how it felt to be fucking her. There was more pounding on the door behind him, the sound of someone's hand flat and frustrated slamming against the thin wood. But he didn't care. He watched Freddie's face as she moved up and down, saw her sucking the blood from his finger until the sounds behind him faded and he became aware only of the beautiful woman on top of him. She arched her back, moving faster, and he let her control him, let her move on him like he was unable to do anything else. She leaned forward, an expression of ecstasy on her face, the skin pulled back against her cheekbones like stretched leather and her tongue rolling against her lips. Felt himself go along with her and begin to explode, reaching up and grabbing her ass so that now he could control her. Lifting her up and off of him and then bringing her crashing back down in a rhythm that grew faster and faster until every muscle in his body contracted and he came in one long shuddering finish. She fell against him, her breasts framing his face, and lay still for a few seconds. Then she whispered, "Did you come for me?"

"I don't even know you."

She shook her head and he could feel the strands of her hair moving gently against the top of his head.

"No, did you *come* for me?"

"Yes."

"*Did* you?"

"Yes."

"You got to shave. We do this again and I want you to shave first."

―᳔᳔᳔᳔―

SHE LAY quietly for several more seconds and then stood up. She pulled her underwear back on and looked in the mirror. "Jesus. Look at me. I look like shit. Don't I look like shit?"

He stood up and gazed at the reflection of Freddie in the mirror. "No, believe me, you don't look like shit."

"I do. Look at me. I'm getting old."

"You're not even, what, twenty-five?"

"I'm closer to thirty than I am to twenty. I mean, I used to be seven years old, I used to be fourteen, and tomorrow I'll be forty or fifty."

"So?"

"I'm dying. Right now. I'm dying. Like a clock. You can hear it. Ticking away."

"You should just split. If you don't want it to be like this that much. Leave."

She smiled and he said, "What?"

"Nothing."

"Come on, tell me."

"There's nothing to tell. Red says I stole money."

"Who's Red?"

"The guy out front. I pointed him out. He says I stole money. Bullshit, that money was coming to me. Your

56

brother found it in the books. Told Red. So I'm his goddamn reward . . . and he's my punishment."

She had an expression on her face as if she was going
to cry, but Jjaks watched her fight it. Took a deep breath
and held it in until she regained her composure. He
wanted to help her out, do something to make her life
seem a little better, but he wasn't sure what. She stared at
him as if she could read his mind and then smiled thinly.
"Fuck it, right?" She pointed at the window behind him.
"You better go that way or there's gonna be a lot of people
wondering what we both were doing in the bathroom for
so long."

He nodded and turned to the window. It opened onto the
side yard and he managed to squeeze through and step out
on the lawn without being seen. Behind him he heard Freddie open the door of the bathroom and say to someone,
"What the hell's the matter with you? Can't a girl do her
thing in the bathroom?"

———

JJAKS WAS moving without thinking about it too much.
He walked out to the bushes by the side of the street
where he had thrown the grocery bag that held his possessions earlier. He pulled a smelly T-shirt out, stuck it in
his back pocket, reached into the bag again, and came
out with a pistol. He stuck that in his back pocket and
started to walk away from his mother's house toward the
center of town.

When he got to the end of the block, he headed to the
right. There was an Exxon station there, run by a guy
named Bob that Jjaks had known as a kid. Jjaks ripped a
couple of eyeholes in the dirty T-shirt, pulled it over his
head, and went inside the station. Bob was sitting behind
the counter and his face went pale when he saw Jjaks. Jjaks
pulled the gun out and said, "Gimme the money."

"Don't shoot."

"I ain't gonna shoot. Just give me the money."

"Wait . . . is that . . . is that Jjaks?"

"Just give me the fucking money."

"You wouldn't shoot me, would you, Jjaks?"

"Goddamn." He shoved the man aside and reached for the cash register. As he went by, the old man grabbed a can of motor oil and hit him on the head with it. Jjaks almost turned and shot him, but at the last second he simply pushed the man over to a closet near the back door of the office, shoved him inside, and locked the door.

He ran to the cash register and looked in the drawer. There was maybe eighty dollars in it. He grabbed that, ran out the front, and stubbed his toe hard against the concrete corner of the wall. He said, "Shit," and started to limp away.

On the way back to his mother's house Jjaks stopped at a gift shop and bought a small gift. He waited while the girl that ran the place wrapped the gift in a small box and put a ribbon on it. He paid with money that had engine-oil stains on it, then thanked her.

When he walked outside he saw a pet shop down the street. He walked over to the plate-glass window in the front of the shop and gazed in. There was a black puppy, a Lab, in a cage that was too small for it right in the front of the window display. Jjaks tapped on the glass and the puppy raised its head, wagged its tail like mad, and stared up at him. Jjaks watched the dog for a long time and then finally turned and headed back to the wedding.

⁓

SAMMY WAS drunk. His tux had purplish-red stains from the cold duck on the front and he was trying to get Freddie to dance with him. He grabbed her and tried to twist her into his arms, but she pushed away from him.

Red was watching and he stepped up to Freddie and told her, "Dance with him."

"You're so fucking concerned," Freddie retorted, "*you* dance with him."

Jjaks appeared at Red's elbow. "If she doesn't want to dance, she doesn't want to dance," he stated. Before anyone could say anything else, Jjaks stepped up to Sammy and held out the gift. He said, "It's a candy dish. Congratulations on your wedding. Good-bye."

Their mother seemed to come out of a trance. "What the hell are you doing?" she cried. "You got no business being snotty." She turned to address the crowd. "He didn't even bring a gift before. I had to tell him to go get one."

"That's right, Nora, you told me to go buy a gift. That's what you said. And it's what I did."

"A candy dish."

"Yes. For my darling older brother."

Sammy yelled, "Jjaks, you can get the fuck out of here. Nobody invited you."

"Our mother did, Sammy," Jjaks returned quietly. He looked at Freddie and saw her mouth move, the words *Don't leave me* form silently, and he said, "I'm sorry." He brushed past her and headed toward the front of the house. He was halfway down the driveway when he heard a loud gasp from the crowd and turned in time to see his mother crumpling to the ground.

Sammy screamed, "Mom," and knelt down, leaning over her. He said, to no one in particular, "Somebody call an ambulance." He looked up as Jjaks came running back and told his brother, "This is your fault."

Jjaks stared at his mother. There was a look of sleepy surprise on her face, like she'd taken a nap in church and farted.

Jjaks remained impassive. "I'll tell you a secret. If I remember right, she probably had too much to drink, that's all."

Sammy shook his head wildly. "She's fucking dead."

Jjaks knelt down and took his mother's hand in his, felt along her wrist for a pulse. There was nothing. He looked over at Sammy, at the tears streaming down his brother's cheeks, and then up at Freddie. She looked like she wanted to take his other hand in hers. He heard Sammy's voice. "You killed her, Jjaks. You killed Mom. I'm gonna get you for this."

Chapter 5

THE CHURCH WAS A huge granite building, with stained-glass windows on three sides. A steeple, above the big, red front door, towered above their car and pointed toward the sky. A large crucifix was planted in the middle of the front lawn as if it had grown there, facing the street. An abstract tree. There was a wrought-iron fence running out back to a cottage, also made of stone, with a new roof, and beyond that, a couple of hundred headstones. No mourners were there besides Sammy and Jjaks.

Sammy said, "I can't believe it. I can't believe she's dead."

"Yeah, it seemed like she'd go on forever. I always thought nothing would stop that woman."

"You could show some respect, not talk about her like she was some kind of machine that ran out of oil and seized up."

"Why should I do that? You think she was something special to me? Jesus, she threw me out of the fucking house

61

when I was a kid." Jjaks thought back to that night, Johnny Cash on the phonograph and his hand feeling like someone had painted it with hot acid. His mother hadn't done a god-damn thing except tell him he ought to quit screaming so loudly.

Sammy said, "She didn't throw you out. She couldn't af-ford to keep us both. She wanted to make sure I got an ed-ucation."

"So you could grow up and keep track of a mobster's money. What a fucking break for you."

"Don't blame me. Mom thought you'd have a better time with Pop. That's all."

"You think that's all? Don't give me that horseshit. I was a little kid. I can tell you what it was like to live with Pop. Half the time I don't believe that man knew who I was and the other half he was kicking my ass all over the place."

Sammy shrugged. They were walking back to the front of the church. Jjaks could see Freddie by Sammy's car. He told Sammy, "The truth is, I don't give a fuck how it makes you feel. Mom dying."

Sammy looked at him with disgust and started to walk back to the car. Jjaks watched him open the gate to the cemetery. There was a huge maple tree over on the edge of the cemetery. It shadowed most of the grounds in the morn-ing sun. He could hear birds up in the branches—crows, he thought, a big one and a baby. The baby bird was calling constantly, an insistent sound interrupted, but not stopped, every few seconds as the mother shoved food down her lit-tle one's throat.

There were wilted flowers at quite a few of the head-stones. Some artificial bouquets too, looking fresh and new. Jjaks wondered, if you knew you'd only get here occasion-ally, was that what you did? Put fake flowers on a grave so they'd hold up better?

As he walked by the church Jjaks noticed that someone had chiseled a date on the cornerstone. Roman numerals,

MCMXXXVIII. He could hear organ music coming from inside. The sound rose and fell with tremendous power. He looked at the stained-glass windows above his head, half expecting them to shatter and shower down on his shoulders.

Jjaks thought maybe the whole thing was stupid, coming here and pretending that the old woman was going to be missed. But for all he knew, maybe Sammy really was broken up about Nora's death.

Jesus, how was he supposed to remember her? It was the only way he thought of her, Nora, ex–Las Vegas showgirl. Almost a stranger to him. When he'd thought of her at all, it was with a mixture of indifference and dislike. He certainly didn't think of her as a mother. Could hardly ever call her Mom. Back in prison he'd known guys who'd broken down, gone crazy from the idea of years behind bars. He'd hear them in their cells at night, weeping and calling out for their mothers. Not only did he not go crazy, but it had never occurred to him to call out for Nora.

There were other times, different times, when it had crossed his mind to call out women's names, run through the list in his head of every woman he'd ever met, the ones he'd fucked and the ones he wished he had. He'd go over them one by one, trying to enjoy it but not get carried away. He'd sit in his cell at night and picture each one naked, with as much detail as he could remember, like who had freckles on their chest, small tits, or big nipples. Try to decide which was the nicest ass and who had the longest legs.

He'd stretch it out for as long as he could, and when he got to the end of the list, he'd start all over again. He thought, looking back on it, even if he *had* gone crazy, he still wouldn't have called out to Nora.

Sammy was waiting by the gate for Jjaks to catch up. "I had to pay the minister. Bribe the son of a bitch. Just to let Mom be buried here and for the asshole to come out and say a few words. I'm talking more than just the cost of the funeral and paying for the plot. Bastard told me, 'Your mother never came to church, I don't know if we have room for her.' The whole time he's got his hand out. Cost me a hundred bucks just to get permission for her to be buried here."

Jjaks said, "Yeah, well, you know how it is with saints. They took that French woman—what was her name, Joan of Arc—they burned her at the stake. So maybe Nora got off lucky."

"You think this is funny?"

"Not funny. If I had to put a word to it, I'd say it was . . . I don't know . . . sad, pathetic? But no, there's nothing funny about any of this."

FREDDIE HAD been watching the two brothers make their way across the cemetery grass. She didn't know what to think. She'd go from looking at Sammy to watching Jjaks, seeing the differences in them and wondering how could they possibly be brothers?

A car pulled up behind her and she saw the cop, Ben Costikyan, get out and saunter over to her. He leaned down and looked into the car.

"Hi, Freddie."

She turned and looked in the other direction. "How's married life been treating you?" he continued. When she didn't say anything he nodded. "That good, huh?" He looked up as Sammy and Jjaks arrived. Jjaks was putting a cigarette in his mouth and Ben smiled at him and asked, "Can I bum one of those?"

Jjaks shook out a cigarette and handed it over. When Costikyan got it lit he shook his head. "Sorry about your mother, boys. Geez, my mother died six years ago. Worst fucking day of my life." He took a drag of his smoke. "I need a word with you, Jjaks."

Sammy laughed. "Why, what'd he do this time?"

Ben put his arm around Jjaks' shoulder as if they were

pals and then spun him hard into the edge of Sammy's car. The sparks from Jjaks' cigarette showered down on the ground and Jjaks grabbed his face in his hands.

Freddie leaned out of the car window and said, "Christ, what'd you do that for?"

Costikyan leaned down and pushed Jjaks with his hand. "So tell me about that gas station you knocked over, Jjaks."

Sammy threw his arms up in the air. He had a look on his face like a parent with a bad child. "It figures."

Costikyan put his knee on Jjaks' back and leaned his weight into it. When he spoke, a little spittle came out of his mouth. "Come on, Jjaks. I could really give a fuck about some shitty little pump stand, but I got a captain downtown that's crawling up my ass for an answer, so I'm here to take a little refuge up yours. That old guy, Bob, he may not have seen you, but he recognized your voice, right?"

Jjaks mumbled, "I don't know what you're talking about."

Costikyan wiped at the spittle on his chin. "It's always something with people like you, Jjaks. Well, we're not finished yet. I want you to know that."

He stood up as if Jjaks wasn't even there any longer, said to Sammy, "My deepest sympathies," and walked back to his car.

——

JJAKS FELL asleep in the spare bedroom of his mother's house only to awake an hour later knowing someone was standing in the doorway. It was Freddie, wearing a thin nightgown. He could see her legs, silhouetted by the light from the hallway.

She walked slowly into the room and sat on the bed.

"Freddie, what are you doing?"

"Shhh. I can't sleep." She put her hand out slowly and rested it on his shoulder. "Did you stay here for me?"

"What?"

"Here, in this house. You were going to go. At the wedding. You gave Sammy the gift and then you said you were leaving."

"I stayed to bury my mother."

Her eyes went down as if she was hurt. "And tomorrow?"

"I'm taking off."

She moved so that her thigh was touching his body and then leaned down and kissed him. He wanted to pull away, not because it didn't feel good but because it didn't make sense. Didn't seem right somehow. But he couldn't. Her lips felt too good against his.

She murmured, "I know you've been thinking about me, Jjaks, because I've been thinking about you. And when I do, I can feel you inside of me. You wanna be inside of me again, Jjaks?"

"We shouldn't . . . again. . . ."

"What shouldn't we do? Fuck? Baby, trust me, we haven't fucked yet."

⁓⁓⁓

SHE TOOK him out to Sammy's car finally because he kept saying that Sammy might wake up any minute and catch them. She looked at him sourly at first and said, "You afraid of what he might do?"

Jjaks answered, "No, I just don't want the hassle."

She took his hand and smiled. "Okay. I know what we can do," and led him out to the driveway where Sammy's car was parked. She opened the door and crawled into the backseat. By the time Jjaks got in, she had her underwear off and was grinning, holding her arms wide and telling him, "Come on, baby."

It had been a long time since Jjaks had fucked anybody in the backseat of a car, but he got the hang of it. His foot got tangled up in the gearshift at first and he had to push the seats forward to get enough room for him and Freddie to lie down.

When he entered her, she arched her back and pushed

against the seat cushion while he braced himself against the folded-down front seat of the car. As they began to rock back and forth it was as if the whole car moved. They clawed at each other and Jjaks thought he heard the oncoming blare of a car horn, but put it out of his mind.

He thrust as far into Freddie as he could, moving her entire body forward in the car until her shoulder bumped the steering wheel and the car horn started to wail.

He could tell she was in the middle of an orgasm, feeling it along the entire length of her body and from the way she clutched him to her. The horn continued to blare, until, finally, she relaxed and fell off of him. She whispered, "I told you to shave."

"Sorry."

There was a moment of silence and then Freddie asked, "Have you ever been to Vegas, Jjaks?"

"No."

"It's the best. I went there once when I was little, with my mother, and we met Ann-Margret. She was so cool, like a kitten with balls. Know what I mean?"

Freddie reached to her neck and pulled up a gold locket so Jjaks could see it.

"She gave me this. She signed her picture and gave me this. It's supposed to bring me luck. Jjaks, let's just go. Let's just start this thing up and take off."

Jjaks looked at her and then glanced away. "I can't."

He opened the car door, stepped out, and began to pull his pants up when he realized that the car was no longer in the driveway. He hadn't imagined that it had moved. It really had. It had rolled down the driveway and was sitting in the middle of the road.

Freddie scrambled out. She pulled up her underpants and said excitedly, "Don't you see? Look at it, it's all there. Maybe all this shit happened—with me, with you, and your mom dying—maybe it all happened so we'd end up together."

Jjaks said slowly, "I can't."

"If you leave me here with these bastards, you are a bigger fucker than they are."

Jjaks gently took her chin, moving her face so she could look directly into his eyes. He told her, "Don't you see? It feels too good, it feels too good. It's gonna turn to shit. I just can't."

She stared at him for a few seconds, then shook her head angrily and marched back toward the house. Jjaks sadly watched her go and then began to push his brother's car back up the driveway.

~~~

JJAKS WENT out that night. He walked through the night without really caring where he was headed and ended up at Grant Industrial Park, acres of parking lot that were all deserted at this time of night. He leaned on the fender of an abandoned car and stared up at the night sky. There were a million stars out.

He heard the sound of an automobile and thought it might be cops, when he realized it was a man and a woman driving out here to enjoy themselves. They were driving a red Camaro. They went right past Jjaks as if they hadn't seen him, and as he watched, the brake lights came on and they coasted to a stop a couple of hundred feet away. The man got out of the car and walked around to the passenger side. He helped the girl out and then together the two of them walked hand in hand into a small field at the far end of the parking lot. Jjaks lifted himself off of the car and watched them carefully. He felt something in his chest, a tightening, some sort of emotion that he wasn't familiar with. He could see the man stop walking and kiss the woman and then the couple disappeared into the tall grass of the field. It made Jjaks want to cry. He felt like going closer, just to see what it was like to be in love. His foot hit gravel and he almost tripped. When he looked down, there seemed to be a thousand stars on the surface of the parking lot. Countless pieces of glass that winked back up at him in the moonlight. Bits of paper blew by in the wind and cigarette butts skittered across the asphalt like scurrying bugs. A small piece of cloth brushed up against Jjaks' shoe and he bent and picked it up. It was lace. He rubbed it thoughtfully with his fingers and it struck him where he'd seen it before. Freddie's veil. Jesus, she'd been running too, before the wedding. Had they brought her out here, chased her down, and then made her go back to Sammy's house? He walked over to the Camaro and opened the driver's side door. The keys were still in the ignition.

Jjaks cut the engine of the Camaro and coasted to a stop outside his mother's house. It was almost pitch-black now; the moon had gone behind the clouds and he had to make his way slowly up to the house and go inside carefully. He was halfway up the stairs when he heard the sound of someone moving around above his head. He stopped and listened as the floorboards creaked. It felt like a silly thing to do, but he pulled the pistol from behind his waist, cocked it, and started up the stairs again.

When he got to the second-floor landing he could see a thin shaft of light spilling into the hallway from Sammy's bedroom. He crept up to the doorway and peered in.

Freddie was moving quietly in the semidarkness, piling clothes into a bag carefully but quickly, as if she didn't want to wake Sammy but didn't want to spend a second longer than she had to inside the house. While Jjaks watched she pulled a picture frame out from under the bed. It was Ann-Margret, with inked-in script across the bottom of the glass. Freddie looked at the picture for a long time and then stuffed it into the bag with her other belongings.

As she was zipping up the bag Jjaks put the pistol back in his waistband again. She saw the movement and whirled in

69

his direction. Her mouth was open and the light reflected brightly off her teeth, making it appear that she was smiling widely. She had pulled her hair back into a ponytail and a strand of it had come loose. It hung down along the side of her face, touching her cheekbone gently and making her seem younger.

She said, "What are you doing back?"

He ignored her. "Where're you going?"

"I don't know. Just 'cause you turned out to be nothing doesn't mean shit. I gotta try."

He took two steps into the room and took her hand in his and backed her into the hallway. Once there, he reached up and touched the tattoo on her arm. Caressed the letters of the word *slut* gently and then said, "Okay."

"Okay what?"

He hesitated. "I got a car outside."

"So."

"Listen to me. I got a car outside."

"What are you saying?"

"You want to go. Let's go."

"You came back for me?" She touched his hand where he had it on her shoulder. "For me?"

He nodded.

She took a step toward him, leaned into his arms, and then gazed up at him. She had an expression on her face as if she was seeing him for the first time.

"You came back for me. You got a car waiting outside. Is that what you're saying?"

"Uh-huh."

"Well, shit, Jjaks." She picked her bag off the floor and linked her arm through his. "What are we waiting for? Let's go."

⁓

JJAKS DIDN'T say much of anything to Freddie after they got in the car. He didn't know what to say. In a way, she was still

70

a stranger. She stared out the windshield while he drove, turning to look at him only once and asking, "I still can't get over the fact that you're Sam's brother?" as if it was too much to believe.

He shrugged. "It's something I try not to remind myself of too often. Why, he forget to mention me?"

She shook her head. "I barely know him except as some creep who works for Red. Sam comes into where I work, where I used to work. Would come in there to stare at me."

Even now, not having time to put on any makeup, she was gorgeous. There was none of that dolled-up quality to her, where you'd see a girl across the street and she'd be a knockout, but when you got closer you'd realize it was all makeup. Get a little closer than that and you'd realize the makeup wasn't even cutting it. Uh-un. This girl was the real thing.

He asked her, "What kind of work do you do?"

She seemed to hesitate before she said, "I dance."

"Dance, huh?" He was looking out the windshield. It had rained and the streets were still slightly wet. Ahead of him was the gift shop and, past that, the pet store where he'd seen the puppy. He pulled over to the curb and turned the car off.

Freddie asked, "What are you doing?"

"I'll be back in a minute."

He got out of the car. There was a heavy metal trash can on the sidewalk and Jjaks picked it up, hefted it onto his shoulder, and threw it through the plate-glass window of the pet shop. From inside the store, the animals woke and the noise of their cries mixed with the piercing sound of the store alarm. From behind him, Jjaks heard Freddie yell, "Jjaks, are you crazy?"

He ignored her and stepped carefully into the window. The black puppy was huddled in its cage, staring up at him with anxious eyes. Jjaks lifted the puppy out of the cage, grabbed a bag of dog food, and said, "It's all right, boy."

When he got back to the car, Freddie's eyes were wild with fear. She was looking around as if she expected the entire Minneapolis police force to descend any second.

Jjaks put the puppy in her lap. "What are you worried about? We did a little shopping is all. Say hello to the pooch."

He started the car up and screeched on down the road. A mile down, he leaned over, opened the glove compartment, and pulled out a bottle of cheap champagne. Freddie looked surprised.

"Came with the car," Jjaks explained, handing the bottle to Freddie.

She popped the cork and champagne sprayed all over the place. They both burst out laughing. But then Freddie said soberly, "They're going to be looking for me, you know."

"I know."

Jjaks, keeping his eyes on the road, turned the radio on. Van Halen was singing "Hot for Teacher." He started to sing softly, humming where he didn't know the words. After a bit Freddie joined in.

⁓

THE FIRST thing Sammy did when he awoke was to reach for Freddie. His eyes snapped open when he realized she wasn't there.

He scrambled out of bed and ran into the hallway, looking for her. By the time he got to Jjaks' bedroom and found out that he was gone too, he realized what had happened.

He ran back to his own bedroom, feeling sick, and snatched the phone out of the cradle. He punched some numbers, waited, and then said, "Yeah, I need to talk to Red, or Joe, I don't care what time it is." He listened and then said, "What do you mean they're out of town? Gimme a number where they are."

He realized he had been hung up on and punched another number into the phone.

When that was answered, he said, "I need Lieutenant Ben—something, Cost—Costikyan, yeah, that's it. . . . Well. Call him at home. It's an emergency? Yeah, it's an emergency. . . . No! Nobody else can help me. Fine, just leave a message."

He hung up and sank down onto the bed with his face in his hands. It couldn't be. It couldn't have happened. Jjaks and Freddie? God wouldn't let that happen to him.

Chapter

7

JJAKS PULLED INTO THE lot of a run-down motel. The place looked ratty as hell, but he didn't have a lot of money. He had a grocery bag with one change of clothing too. No sense forgetting that.

"Where you going?" Freddie asked.

"In here." He pointed to a space by the motel office. They stopped and he said, "I don't know, we could go downtown, see if they got a room at the Hilton, but I thought I'd try here first. 'Less you got a better idea?"

The place had weeds in the parking lot and a busted sign above the office door that advertised cable TV and rates by the day or week. There was an area of newer paint waist-high, about twenty square feet, just beyond the office door. It appeared that somebody had started to fix the place up at some point but had run out of paint, or ambition. The building was on a corner lot, sandwiched between a one-way street and a dry cleaners that had gone out of business. The far end of the lot was enclosed by chain-link fence that

74

ended just before a ten-foot-high, graffiti-covered wall. The only way in or out was the way Jjaks and Freddie had just come.

The neighborhood had an aura of long-term hopelessness about it during the day. A feeling that nothing was going to happen that hadn't already occurred dozens of times before. There was a sense of not-so-hidden danger too, as if the area could ignite into violence with little provocation.

Freddie shut the engine off. She looked at Jjaks. "You're broke? God, I should have known. It's the story of my life. Men with no money, or men with a lot of money who don't let me have any of it."

He grinned, dug in his pocket, and came up with some crumpled bills. "Not broke. Yet. I might be in a day or two." He took a cigarette out of the pack in his shirt and tried flipping it into his mouth. It hit his chin and bounced off onto the ground.

Freddie watched him try it again with the same results. "Jesus, save me from country boys," was her only comment.

He looked at the clothes she was wearing. "Honey, I got to say, you aren't exactly impressing me. Unless you got money in one of your pockets, looks like we're gonna have to enjoy the hospitality of this fine establishment."

It took a second, with her looking at his face like she was seeing him for the first time since they'd left his mother's house, but she smiled finally and grabbed his arm. "Listen, you've got to tell me something. I've got to know you'll help me. Somehow, you got to help me."

"Help you do what?"

"Whatever. I'll let you know."

On the way to the motel office she slid her hand down through his arm and asked, "This place have showers?"

"I hope so."

"You really are Sam's brother?"

"Uh-huh."

75

"And you and I, we just met yesterday, and between us, we've got a few dollars and some change. Holy shit."

She started to laugh softly. He stopped walking and asked, "What now?"

"Must be my lucky day, is all."

―⁓⁓―

BY THE time they got the room, it was too late to go to sleep. They went and got a cup of coffee at a refreshment kiosk by the pool.

Inside the kiosk was an old twenty-five-cent photo booth. Jjaks sat in a chair while Freddie held the puppy and sat on Jjaks' lap.

Jjaks put a quarter in the machine, blinked into the flash, and waited while the photo strip came out. He stared at the pictures. They looked like photos of a happy family. In the background you could see the motel pool and the edge of a tree. If you got past the peeling paint in the pool, the scene looked idyllic.

Jjaks said, "I promised myself, I gotta turn my life around. I have to do things differently. So, is this doing things differently? Running off with someone else's wife?"

"You can't look at it like that."

Jjaks turned to Freddie. "How else can you look at it?"

He'd dropped the photos and realized that the puppy was starting to chew on them. As he snatched the strip away Freddie said, "I mean, look at it like this. Time is . . . like an orange. It's round. Everything gets repeated and all things that are supposed to happen happen for a reason."

They got up out of the kiosk and wandered over to the pool. It was chilly outside and there was sludge in the bottom of the pool, but they sat side by side on a ratty-looking lounge chair. The puppy settled itself under the chair.

Freddie said, "Okay, so it's bullshit. But here we are, and it's not so bad."

They both looked around. Freddie shrugged. "Okay, so it

stinks. But it's going to get better . . . if you just listen to me."

"The big promise I made to myself," Jjaks said, "was that I would never spend another day in prison, not one."

Freddie said, "The truth is, quit sticking up gas stations. That'll keep you out of prison."

She moved closer to him and began to undo his belt.

Jjaks said, "What are you doing?"

"Relax." She untied her hair ribbon, shook out her hair, and tied the thin piece of ribbon around Jjaks' neck like a keepsake. Then she pushed at him until he was lying on his back in the lounge chair. She crawled on top of him and lowered herself gently, pressing her body along the length of his.

She watched his eyes close in pleasure. Out of the corner of her eye, she saw movement and realized there was a woman in the manager's office watching them. It excited Freddie, knowing they were being observed. She stared back at the woman, leaned back, and slowly unbuttoned her jacket and then her shirt, revealing her breasts.

Freddie put her hand down the front of her pants and touched herself, smiling and then winking at the wide-eyed, nosy woman in the office. She said to Jjaks, "We're going to have so much fun." Then she leaned over and took him in her mouth.

AFTERWARD FREDDIE and Jjaks went inside and Jjaks played with the puppy while Freddie took a shower.

She came out of the shower with a towel wrapped around her and another one in her hands, scrubbing her hair vigorously. Jjaks watched.

The room was painted a light pink. It had a black-and-white television bolted to a Formica counter and a big, brown-spotted mirror directly across from the bed. Underneath the counter was a drawer that held half of a city phone book and a Bible that appeared to have been bled on in the past. The wall was cracked, a big line running like the Mississippi River, from floor to ceiling. There was a cockroach in the corner that hadn't moved since they'd arrived. Reminded Jjaks of a pet he'd had back in the federal pen.

While she was in the shower he listened to the sound of the water and tried to decide what he was going to say when she walked out. There were several possible scenarios. He replayed them in his mind.

What he could do, he could be sitting there, looking out the window or watching TV, not paying a lot of attention. When she walked out, he could act surprised, say, "You have a good time in there?" Ask her if she felt clean now. Or else, and this might work, he could pretend to fall asleep. He practiced lying on the bed while she was in the bathroom. Or, he could just act tired and say, "You done *already*? I must have dozed off."

The truth was, he didn't know what to say. She was his brother's wife, for one thing. And for another, she was the first woman he'd been alone with in over four years. At one point he looked down at his crotch and said, "You all right about this? Can you take all of this excitement?" It was giving him more than a little to think about.

Now Freddie stood in front of the mirror and bent sideways, pulling at her hair and giving little grunts of concentration. Her hair looked darker and longer when it was wet. He watched the edge of the towel where it was wrapped around her thighs. Got a quick peek of something soft. She caught his look in the mirror and stopped. "What?"

He smiled. Behind him the air conditioner was going full blast, making a lot of noise but not producing much cold air. Watching Freddie, he felt like he was in the middle of a heat wave. He had an idea, from a feeling he was getting, that he didn't have to worry if his privates were gonna be up to it. He was getting his answer to that already.

78

Earlier, Jjaks had walked across the street to a bar and bought a six-pack of Budweiser beer. The puppy had followed him and now it sat on the floor by his feet, watching every move Jjaks made.

Jjaks said, "Go away." It sat on its hind legs and cocked its head. Jjaks had an open can of beer in one hand and had taken his shirt off. He took a cigarette out and flipped it up toward his mouth. Tried to catch it in his teeth but couldn't. He tried again and hit himself in the forehead. Finally he gave up and put the cigarette carefully in his mouth.

The puppy was playing with the bedspread. Freddie took one look at the dog and made a kissing sound. She said, "Hey, pooch," and then went back to combing her hair.

Jjaks saw her glance in the mirror at his chest. He felt like he was on display, so he pulled the sheet over his waist and tried to pretend that he was used to being in motel bedrooms with half-naked women.

He asked, "How'd you get so dirty? The other day at the wedding?"

"I was out jogging."

"What'd you do, run to your own wedding?"

She laughed. "You think they've got a place in that book? *Guinness World Records,* whatever it's called. Shortest marriage in history. You think I'll be in there? Me and your brother?"

"I don't think so. For one thing, you're still married."

"Not in my head, I'm not. Never was."

"Well, your head is one thing. Legally is something else. You're still married."

"Not for long."

He took a pull from the beer can. "You want to tell me what the hell was that all about? You marry my brother. The man's an asshole, excuse me if he is your husband now. He's still an asshole."

She stepped away from the mirror. Her hair was still wet, little droplets of water running off the ends of it and staining the towel. He sat where he was, trying to be nonchalant, but aware of how small the towel was at the same time. Back in jail, he used to look at magazines, think about what it would be like to spend time with a beautiful girl. He couldn't think of any, back then, that had been as sexy as this one.

Their eyes locked in the mirror through the steam, like Tarzan seeing Jane through the jungle mist. Jjaks could feel her eyes on him like they were two stars on a clear night. Suddenly all he wanted to do was fuck her again. It came over him like a wave. He could tell she knew what he was thinking.

She sauntered over to the bed. He didn't know what she was seeing. She acted like she was the main event in a smoke-filled World War II café in Paris, or the back streets of bombed-out London, and the room was full of the 82nd Airborne about to drop behind enemy lines the next day at dawn. She was putting on a show, moving to some kind of music that only she heard, while Jjaks sat in silent appreciation.

When she got to the edge of the bed, she stood still for a minute and then let the towel drop. He swallowed some of the beer the wrong way and had to cough, take a few seconds to come up with enough air to keep on breathing.

When he regained his breath, she told him. "The whole thing is a long story. I stole some money. That's what they said, even if it isn't true. So, for punishment, I had to marry your brother. If you want me to tell you, I could talk about what it would be like, married to your brother. Or, you got anything else you might want to do?" She pointed at the sheet. "Looks to me like you were thinking of going camping, pitching a tent right there under that sheet."

―――

LATER SHE asked him, "Do you believe in love at first sight?"

Jjaks was stroking her hair, watching the lights from outside the motel room peek through the curtains and reflect off her face.

He said, "I don't know. I'm not sure I believe in love at all."

"Oh, come on. You never saw a woman, spent time with her, and fell in love?"

"Not that I recall. I spent time with a woman once, in Pittsburgh. I'd sit in front of her Sony Trinitron, watch the Steelers play."

"Did you love her?"

"I don't think so. She was fun. But when I finally left I didn't miss her. I don't believe I loved her."

She nestled her head into his arms, pressed against his chest, and murmured, "Poor baby."

"No, it was all right. I think I was just tired of her."

"That's not what I meant."

"I know that."

"Well, if you don't think you want to fall in love . . ."

"I didn't say that."

"Yeah, all right, but if you're not looking for it, or if it never happened, what *do* you want?"

"I just don't want to go to jail. That's all. I promised myself, I said, I gotta turn my life around. Do things differently."

"Well, here we are."

He fell asleep like that, holding on to her and listening to her breathe. Thinking about what had happened since he'd walked through the penitentiary gates. Jesus. He came home, went to a wedding, pissed off a local mobster, and stole his brother's wife. A busy fucking day.

Something stirred. The mattress shifted as Freddie moved slowly off the bed. Jjaks kept his eyes half-closed, listening. She had a red mark across her butt from where she'd been lying on the bed. It reminded him of the mark on his own hand, the tattoo of the burner that Sammy had given him as a going-away present all those years ago.

He waited to see what she was going to do. He thought she might leave, bolt into the quiet of the night so that he'd wake up to an empty room. He thought that if she did, he might regret it, feel lonely in the morning. But he wasn't going to do anything to stop her.

Jjaks sat up suddenly. Freddie went back to the bed. She was naked and she touched his arm, stroking his skin lightly. He could feel it all the way up to the ends of his hair. She said, "I didn't want to wake you. I was thinking."

"About what?"

"I know how we can do this, get more money."

"How?"

"You're talking about not going back to prison. I'm talking about something different. I'm saying all you have to do is go back home one last time. Go back one time and get some money."

"What money?"

"There's money there, I know it. I can't take the chance of going back. . . . That means you have to."

"Why? We have a little cash and—"

"Sure, I got this fifty bucks I keep stuffed in my underwear and you got what? Enough to spring for a swell place like this. Sammy has money. We left in a hurry. I forgot."

"So?"

"Jjaks, c'mon, we're almost there. *Almost*. It's like if I close my eyes, I can see us at Caesars. Wait till you lay your eyes on that place, it's got the biggest swimming pool in the world and all the towels smell like Downy Fabric Softener. It's all white, like a desert palace—always sunny and warm. And when I get going there, I can float in the pool every day and get a real nice tan, we can together, and you'll come see me perform at night and I'll come off stage and I'll be too wired to sleep, so we'll make love until morning and then fall asleep until two."

She reached over and held his hand, looked into his eyes, and kissed him softly and deeply. "Look, it's half my money,

82

right? I'm his wife, right? That's the law. He kept saying that he was gonna make me happy, that he had all this money stashed away. So, after everything, let him make me happy. Jjaks . . . I just don't know where he hides it."

She leaned into him so that he could feel her breast pressing against his shoulder, put her mouth to his ear, and whispered, "Baby, come on. This isn't breaking the law. It's your brother. He's the one who broke the law. He forced me to marry him." She put her hand on his crotch. "C'mon, we're almost there. Almost." Her eyes seemed to get brighter. She sat up on the bed. "Jjaks, just think of Vegas."

He thought of his mother and said softly, "I know all about Vegas."

"It's like I can close my eyes and see myself at Caesars. See both of us."

"I know."

"Jjaks, I want to dance there. I don't want to waste my time dancing in these shitty little clubs around here. I want to go out to Vegas and dance there."

She got up off the bed and walked to the window. Her body was in the shadows now, silhouetted against the drapes. To Jjaks it appeared as if he was watching someone in the next room, a woman who didn't know she was being observed and was pacing back and forth on the other side of the curtain.

She said, "Look, it's half my money now anyway, right? I mean, I'm his wife now. What's his is mine. That's the law. He kept saying he wanted to make me happy, so now's his chance." She stopped pacing. "I just have to find out where he hides it."

Jjaks was overcome with a memory suddenly, staring at Freddie and thinking about the money she was talking about. He could picture his brother, twenty-three years before, hiding things, old copies of *Playboy* and money he stole from their mother.

Freddie must have seen something on his face because

83

she smiled. "You *know*. You know where he hides things, don't you?"

He took his time answering, not wanting to commit himself, but then plunging ahead because he couldn't think straight with her standing naked in front of him. He nodded slowly and tried grinning at her. "I know . . . I know where he used to hide things."

She had an expression on her face like she was trying to thread a needle in the dark. Intent. He thought about his situation. His mother was dead. He didn't like his brother, so there was nothing holding him to this place. Fuck Sammy. Last time he'd seen his brother, Sammy'd held Jjaks' hand over a hot stove.

That thought helped him make up his mind. But he didn't want to run into anything. He wanted to approach it the right way, get some facts first. He asked Freddie, "Sammy has money?"

"Yes. Sammy has money. He's got a shitload of cash."

"Yeah?"

She put her hand on her heart. "Honest."

"I could use some money."

She squealed and ran over to him. "Oh, baby, that's more like it. You'll see, we'll head out to Vegas. You and I. I'll make you the happiest man alive."

Chapter 7

JJAKS PULLED THE CAR up just past his brother's house. The moon was out, making it bright enough to see across the yard to the front door. Where he'd parked, though, everything was in shadows.

He sat there for a while, thinking the thing through. What were the chances that he'd get in, find the money, and get out? Instead, what if he started the car, headed toward Wisconsin, or why not Canada? Head north and be there in a couple of hours. Could he make it before he ran out of money to buy gas?

Jjaks was pretty sure he was right. Thinking back to twenty-five years before when he was still living with his mother and brother. Sammy had a hiding place that he thought no one knew about. He'd pried up a section of the floorboards. Kept loose change and porn magazines in there. Jjaks had seen him one night. Sammy must have thought everyone was asleep and he'd lifted the boards up. Sammy was dumb enough to still use the same hiding place.

Jjaks could hear the cicadas in the trees and had to ask himself, if they were the only things up and stirring, what was he doing out here? There was wetness to the air, more than humidity. He had the feeling he'd just missed a big storm, one of those summer thundershowers that burst quickly and violently but didn't leave much of a trace when they were over. It could have rained here and not back at the motel. Or else, he had so much on his mind that he hadn't noticed when it did rain.

He thought of Freddie. What was she doing right now? Waiting for him to get back with the money. Maybe she was taking another shower. Drying her hair. There was no reason for her to be doing anything except for waiting.

He knew he was going to go into the house and give it a try. All he had to do was get in and out before anybody even knew he was in the neighborhood.

It probably wasn't the best time, but he couldn't help wondering about the circumstances behind Freddie marrying his brother. Freddie had told him that she'd stolen money from Red. But to make her marry Sammy, what kind of punishment was that?

Jjaks made up his mind. It wasn't going to do anybody any good if he spent the night in a car outside his brother's house. May as well get it over with.

He got out of the car and made his way silently to the house. The porch was rotting. He put some weight against the railing, felt it move, start to give way. He yanked his hand off and froze. Behind him, a couple of houses away, a dog started to bark.

There was a lawn mower on the far side of the porch. For a second Jjaks had a crazy desire to go over and start it up. He could get it going, let it roar into the silence of the night. Be out back cutting the grass when Sammy came stumbling out. Maybe they could chat when he was done mowing the lawn. Get over their past differences.

It took a minute for the thought to go away. Jjaks had to

shake his head, get his concentration back. He was about to break into the house. There was no time for lunatic fantasizing about cutting grass or socializing.

The front door was unlocked and he slipped inside, making his way to the corner of the living room where Sammy used to hide his dirty magazines. It was still there, the trapdoor with the small safe that had a combination lock on it. He squinted into the darkness, trying to recall the combination but couldn't. He was stuck; what was he going to do, hope he got lucky? His gaze moved to the hallway, to where a framed portrait of his mother hung. She was in her chorus outfit and Jjaks suddenly remembered what was on the back of the frame. Sammy had a lousy memory and he'd long ago written the combination on the back of that picture. Jjaks crept over and looked. There it was. Sammy was still dumb enough to leave it where somebody could get at it.

Jjaks opened the safe, reached in, and came up with an envelope full of cash. He had no idea how much was there, but it was more than he'd had five minutes before. All he had in mind now was to get the fuck out of there.

———

SAMMY REACHED slowly for the phone in his bedroom. He pushed the numbers for Ben Costikyan's house and waited. He could hear Jjaks out in the living room fumbling around in the dark. It wasn't a thing that surprised Sammy. Why should it, everything else had been like this, what was so different with his own brother coming back to rip him off?

Costikyan came on the line. "What?"

"Ben . . . Lieutenant . . . you told me to call back. He's here. Jjaks."

"He alone?"

"I think so."

"You *think* so?"

Sammy spoke quickly. "Yeah, yeah, he's here alone."

87

"Well, make sure he doesn't leave. I'll be over."

Sammy hung up and thought about what the cop had said. Make sure Jjaks doesn't leave. He got up out of his bed and knelt on the floor, reached his arm under the bed, and pulled out his pistol.

The black metal of the gun gleamed in the moonlight. He smiled. He'd make sure Jjaks didn't go anywhere.

——

JJAKS STOOD up from the safe slowly, ready to turn, and felt the cold metal of a gun barrel against the side of his head.

Sammy said, "Shit, you really think I'd fall for it? You two could have done better than that."

Jjaks said, "I guess I made a mistake coming here."

"Hell, boy, you made a mistake coming here the first time, yesterday. You'll pay for it. You come home, take my bride, and try to steal my money."

"Freddie said it wasn't your money."

"She did? Well, I got some news for you. Freddie doesn't know what she's talking about."

"I'll tell you what, I'll put the money back. We can forget about it. Then I'll walk out that front door and you'll never see me again."

"Yeah? You kill your mother. My mother. Make her drop dead of a heart attack, and now you're here to steal from me."

"Sure. I came back to see if she left me anything in the will, huh?"

"You think it's funny? Your own mother died."

"Well, maybe I've got a different perspective on it. I hadn't seen much of her lately, you know what I mean?"

"You want to joke about it?"

Jjaks smiled. "It just hasn't sunk in yet. I'm in shock. Any minute, I'm gonna burst out in tears."

"You killed her."

"I didn't kill her."

88

"Bullshit. And now I'm gonna kill you."

"Why don't you do this? Let me out the front door. I'll put the money back and really never come back."

"Sure. And then you and *my* wife can live happily ever after. Sounds like a good deal for me."

"We're gonna go at it, aren't we, Sammy? Yes, we are."

Sammy took a step back but still held the gun only inches from Jjaks' ear. "Where's Freddie?"

Jjaks decided, fuck it, he didn't feel like putting up with his brother's shit anymore. "Who?"

"Goddamm it, where is she?"

"You remember, when we were kids, Mom gave me away, sent me to live with Dad?"

"So what? You going to cry about it?"

"That same day, you held my hand down on the fucking stove."

"Jesus."

"I told myself I wasn't ever going to forget."

"You want me to go in the kitchen, turn on the stove so we can play chicken?"

Jjaks smiled. "No. I just want you to know why I'm gonna beat the fuck out of you." And then he looked past Sammy and said, "Hey, Freddie," to the air, waiting for Sammy to look. Jjaks knew there was no way Sammy wouldn't. He timed it, gave Sammy an instant to turn his head, and then lashed out with his fist, knocking the gun out of his brother's hand.

Sammy gave a yell and swung back, in time for Jjaks to hit him squarely on the chin. Jjaks felt something snap in his hand, like he'd fractured a knuckle. He didn't think about it. Instead, he took a step toward Sammy and hit him again. Sammy grabbed him as he went down. Together they rolled on the floor, trading punches.

Jjaks got Sammy's head in his arm and tried to break the floorboards with it. He could hear Sammy cursing, the steady chant of "motherfucker, motherfucker" coming from him as if it was his personal mantra.

Somehow, Sammy slipped out of Jjaks' grasp and locked his hands around Jjaks' throat. Jjaks spit in Sammy's face and tried to knee him in the crotch. He missed. Sammy leaned into Jjaks' face. For a second Jjaks thought his brother was gonna kiss him. But Sammy didn't kiss him, he moved his head to the side and closed his teeth on Jjaks' ear.

Jjaks screamed with a pain that he hadn't felt since Sammy held his hand over the burner. He clutched his ear, felt Sammy pull away, and realized with horror that his brother had a part of his ear in his mouth. He grabbed at Sammy's face, tore his own earlobe out of Sammy's mouth, and began to hit him as hard as he could.

He was a machine, feeling nothing but pain and fury, pummeling Sammy until the man collapsed like a dead man, trying to cover his head with his hands. Jjaks kept punching until his arms got tired.

When his rage had subsided, Jjaks picked up the envelope of cash. He could feel blood pouring down his face, covering his shoulders and shirt. With a grunt, he walked over to Sammy, tore his brother's shirt off, and held it against his own head, trying to stop the flow of blood. Then he went to the front door and wrenched it open.

⁓

JJAKS RAN out as Lieutenant Costikyan was screeching into the driveway. Jjaks hid behind the bushes and waited. When Costikyan walked by, he leaped out and grabbed him behind the neck. He ran him headfirst into the hood of his police car, smashing the man into a headlight. He heard the sound of glass breaking and ran Costikyan into the light on the other side of the car and sent the lieutenant sprawling to the ground.

Money from the envelope had spilled out and Jjaks scrambled on the ground, trying to scoop up as much of the cash as he could in the dark. A pint bottle of whiskey had fallen out of Costikyan's pocket and Jjaks scooped it up and tucked it in the waist of his pants. He looked down at the crumpled figure of the cop and smiled. ". . . take a little refuge up yours."

Inside, he could hear Sammy shouting and the sound of furniture crashing. Jjaks could feel pain, like a river of fire running from his ear down the length of his neck, and had to ignore it. Had to concentrate on getting out of there instead.

He scooped a couple more bills into his pockets and took off for his car.

―⁓⁓―

SAMMY CLAYTON got to his feet after Jjaks had left and stumbled out to his car. He saw Lieutenant Costikyan lying on the ground. He leaned down. "Lieutenant?" He pushed at him. "Yo, Lieutenant."

The man's face was bloody. When he didn't respond, Sammy looked up and down the street and then stepped back and kicked the lieutenant in the stomach. "I never did like you, you son of a bitch." He ran down to his car and hopped in.

Turning the key, he hit the gas and the car flooded. He said, "Fuck," and tried again, twisting the key and rocking in the seat like he was part of the engine. Shouting, "Come on, come on," until, finally, the engine fired and the car roared to life. He backed out, threw the car into drive, and raced down the street.

He caught up to Jjaks five minutes later. It was easy as hell. All he did was head down the main drag into town and he almost ran him over. Jjaks had stopped at a store to buy smokes and was making his way back across the street to his car. He was stumbling across the intersection while cars honked at him.

Sammy coasted to a stop and watched while Jjaks got into

his car and drove erratically away from the store. He followed Jjaks down Capers Street and waited while Jjaks paused at an intersection and then swung a wild left onto Devault. He turned right, into a gas station, without signaling. Sammy had to stop fifty feet away to find out what his brother was up to.

Jjaks got out of the car and went directly into the men's room of the gas station. Sammy waited for the door to close behind Jjaks and then bolted across the street to a phone booth. He dialed 911 and waited. When it was picked up on the other end, he yelled into it, "I'm calling about Ben Costikyan. I just saw it. He got beat up. That's right. It was Jjaks Clayton that did it. He beat the hell out of Costikyan." He slammed the phone down and ran back to his car. He was about halfway there when a horse trailer pulled into the station. It was white and red, pulled by a big Dodge diesel truck, with lettering, CLEMENTINE, THE DANCING HORSE, in white script along the side of the van. Sammy watched as the station attendant went out to the trailer and began filling it with gas. The man driving the van got out to talk with the attendant.

Sammy was still trying to come up with some way to foil Jjaks' plans as Jjaks himself stepped out of the bathroom. He had cleaned himself up a bit but still looked like a bloody mess. He was drinking from the bottle he'd picked up, holding his head way back and putting the bottle to his lips. He started to make his way to his car.

Sammy ran back to his own car only to find that he'd locked the keys inside. He panicked. He could try to pick the lock, but by then, Jjaks could have gone anywhere.

Jjaks was already in his car, starting up. As Sammy watched he coasted out of the station and started up the street. Jjaks was weaving between lanes and Sammy watched him clip a trash can, sending it bouncing into a building.

Sammy did the only thing he could think of. He ran

across the island, out of sight of the attendant, and hopped into the horse trailer. The keys were in the ignition. Without further thought, he started it up and took off. He heard a loud snap behind him as the hose from the gas pump broke. The attendant swore and the driver of the van yelled out loudly, "Hey, that's my horse. That's Clementine."

Sammy saw the two of them in his rearview mirror and for an instant he almost stopped. But then he caught a glimpse of Jjaks careening down the street and he hit the gas. There was thump from the back and a neigh. Sammy rolled down the window and screamed out, "Hang on to your socks, Clementine."

———

FREDDIE ASKED, "This is it?" She was staring at the small pile of bills on the motel bed, giving him a look like he had to be kidding. "Is this a joke?"

His hand was killing him from punching Sammy. Actually, his entire body wasn't feeling too good. His adrenaline was still pumping, but he was trying to calm down. Sure as hell, he didn't want to talk about what had happened.

Jjaks said, "What are you talking about? That's all he had."

Jjaks was still holding his brother's blood-soaked shirt to his head. He'd been gulping the whiskey ever since he'd left Sammy's house. Right now he felt like he was gonna puke from the whiskey and his ear still hurt.

He said, "Look at what he did to me."

She took her eyes off the cash and glanced at his face. "Are you all right?"

He took a long drink of the whiskey and coughed. "Jesus." He took the shirt away from his ear.

"Oh, my God." She leaned in close to him. "What did he do?"

Jjaks tried to grin. "He bit my ear off. That son of a bitch bit my goddamn ear off."

93

"Why'd he do that?"

"I don't know. Maybe the motherfucker was hungry." He put the bottle down and started to dig through his pockets. "Wait . . . I got it right here."

"Got what?" She was still staring at the side of his head, with a look of disgust.

"I got it." Grabbing something wet and spongy, he pulled the bottom end of his ear out in triumph. "Here it is. I wasn't going to leave it there. No way. Maybe we can tape it back on."

"You're drunk."

"Not as drunk as I want to be."

"God, you're drunk, you got your ear bit off, and you didn't get most of the money."

"I got to wash up." He lurched to his feet and stumbled into the bathroom with Freddie right behind him. He turned the water on and started splashing his face, picking at the dried blood.

She came up behind him and peered at his reflection in the mirror. "You need a doctor."

"I don't need a doctor." He gazed at her from under his arms.

"Are you sure? You don't look good."

"I'm fine." But he wasn't. His head was starting to pound and he was dripping sweat now. He could feel it on his forehead and running down his arms. "I've got a little fever, is all."

"You're pale as a ghost."

"Yeah?"

She nodded and then reached out to touch his forehead. "Jjaks, you're burning up."

He was. He was also thinking it wasn't a bad way to get her sympathy. "I don't feel great, if that's what you're asking."

His stomach heaved again and he tasted bile. Forcing it down, he turned away from her toward the sink. What he ought to do was get in bed and finish that bottle of whiskey. Let her feel a little sorry for him.

There was sweat in his eyes. He felt her hand on his arm. "I have to get a doctor for you. I'm serious."

"No, I throw up when I go to the doctor. Every time."

"You sure?"

He turned to her, ready to tell her that he was okay. He opened his mouth to say it, seeing the look on her face, concerned. Thinking it was an improvement over fury. And then he threw up all over her shoes.

He had just enough time to see her back away from him and say, "Goddammit, Jjaks."

And then he vomited again.

*

WHEN HE was done he wiped his face and looked at Freddie. "Sorry."

"God, you're a mess. You're disgusting." She took her shoes off and threw them in the bathtub. "Do you always do this, go on a simple errand and come back more dead than alive?"

"What are you talking about? I got it." He pointed to the pile of crumpled bills. "No problem."

"Bullshit." She walked back into the room and he trailed after her. "Sammy had more. I saw it. He had fifty thousand bucks. What do you have here, a couple of hundred?"

"What about my ear?"

"I'm sorry about your ear."

He cupped his hand to the side of his face, tried grinning, and said, "*What*?"

"You think there's time for kidding around?"

"Got a better idea?"

She stood up and began to pace back and forth. "Jjaks, you don't get it. I need that money. I'm sorry about your ear, but we've got to figure a way to get more money."

"Not me."

"What do you mean? All you've got to do is go back in that house and get the cash. He's got loads of it, hidden away." She stopped pacing and said, "Jjaks, I earned that goddamn money, all the shit I've been through."

"I'm not going back in there. I already did and I ran into a problem. Two problems."

"What?"

"Well, for one thing, my brother."

"I'll call him, get him out of there."

"What if I had gotten shot?"

She gave him a look, innocent, and said, "But you didn't."

"Right. And what the fuck was the cop, Costikyan, doing there? How come he was waiting for me outside? I almost killed him."

"I don't know."

"You don't know? He's gonna have a headache when he wakes up."

"You . . . you didn't kill him, did you?"

"Shit. I'll tell you what. If I had, I wouldn't've come back here. I'd be headed out of the state. Go back to Pittsburgh and see if Terry Bradshaw came out of retirement. You can take that to the fucking bank."

She stalked back to the bed and picked up a couple of dollar bills. "You call this a score?"

"It's as good as it's gonna get tonight."

She threw the bills down again, only to pick them up immediately, and said, "I sent you out there and all you do, you fuck it up so bad and get your ear chewed off in the bargain." She started to yell. "I counted on you, Jjaks, how could you let this happen?"

"It wasn't my fault."

He thought she was going to start crying, but the expression on her face changed to anger as he watched. Silent tears, streaming down her face, all of a sudden—not sobbing—only tears. She was too busy being furious, with a "why me?" look on her face. It was more anger than he'd expected.

Jjaks said, "Wait a minute. . . ." Seeing it as a problem, something to be smoothed over. But nothing more than that, at first.

She screamed, "You wanna tell me—take your time about it," holding the bills in the air, "tell me why this is all you got? I know Sammy has more. I know it."

This should've been hysterical. Or something. He was down to one ear, looked like he'd been made up for a low-budget horror flick, nothing but blood on his head. They should both be laughing. Or getting drunk. Drunker. But she wasn't laughing, and unless she stopped crying long enough to listen, he wouldn't be laughing either.

It crossed his mind to walk out, leave, go somewhere and wait for her to calm down. He could call her in the morning. Tell her he had thought it best to let things cool down. Because he wasn't up for this, a fight. He just wanted it to go away, the whole scene. He couldn't believe it had gone even this far.

She took a step forward, thrusting the money in his face. Now she was spitting on him as she talked, little flecks of saliva hitting him on his cheek. She was moving closer and closer until there was no room between them. He could feel her chest against his, the weight of her breasts pushing into him—a feeling that he almost enjoyed.

He'd fallen in love with them—her breasts. They were small, but still, he loved to touch them. If things were different, if they weren't yelling at each other, he could picture touching them. What he'd do, he'd sneak up behind her, reach around, and squeeze them. Surprise her when she wasn't expecting it. It had been a helluva night and he wouldn't mind getting right back in bed with her. Do something to make the pain go away. They could go to bed. He'd play with her breasts some more and then they'd fuck.

But it wasn't like they were gonna fuck now. Maybe not

97

ever again, not the way it looked from where he stood, with her holding the money an inch and a half away from his nose and yelling, "Go on, tell me what the hell this is. Tell me what it's called."

"It's money. Not a lot. But it's the best I could do." Getting it right, the tone of voice, flat, so she wouldn't react to it the wrong way. It was what he wanted, keep everything low-key. He said it again, "It's money, that's all."

She pulled her hand back and threw the bills at him. They felt like they cut his face, hitting him that hard. He bent down and picked them up while she silently watched.

"What?"

"Jesus, Freddie, wait . . . this is all there was." He was lying again but didn't want to admit he'd dropped most of the cash in his fight with Sammy. "Maybe your information was wrong."

"My information wasn't wrong. Sammy showed it to me the other day when he was trying to talk me into marrying him. Trying to impress me." She took a step backward. "This is my last chance. This is it. I'm not a young girl anymore. You think I want to dance in those fucking nightclubs, wave my tits in the air so some douche bag can stick a dollar bill in my crotch? Is that what you think?"

"No."

"So, maybe it's all right with you. You think you can live on fifty bucks. Is that what you think, Mr. Cool, nothing bothers me, Jjaks-goddamn-Clayton, who acts like everything's perfect?"

"We'll get more."

"Is that all you can say, we'll get more? Jesus Christ, Jjaks, this isn't a game. This isn't something you're watching on TV. You can't sit back and pretend it doesn't have anything to do with you."

"I know."

"You know? God. Why don't you try to get a little concern in your voice. I don't think you know anything. I don't think you know what the hell's going on." She took a step toward him, real close again. "See, I hear the words come out, you trying to act, what, normal? If someone was listening, maybe he'd think they were the right words. Fucking appropriate, whatever. You're saying what you think I want to hear."

He said, "Freddie, this whole thing—you're blowing it way out of proportion. Tomorrow will be better. You'll see." He didn't want it to go any further. She was right about that. He wanted to forget about it. Tell her, Freddie, let's put it aside. We don't have to talk the thing to death. It's what he wanted to say, but he didn't.

He said, "We're doing fine. . . ."

"Yeah? You know what, the sad thing is, you probably think we are."

"Shit . . ."

She took a deep breath, sucked a lot of air into her lungs, and then screamed, "You wanna tell me how goddamn fine we're doing. I married your fucking brother yesterday, for Christ's sake. And now here I am, stuck in some shitty motel room with you. And you aren't looking that good to me either." She slapped him in the face. "You wanna tell me that, you son of a bitch?"

———

SHE THREW herself at him, shoving him hard enough that he dropped his bottle of whiskey. It surprised him so much that he reacted instinctively. He bounced back up off the floor and shoved her into the wall.

There was a moment of silence and then someone pounded on the wall from the next room and yelled, "Cut it out, I'll call the goddamn manager if you don't shut the hell up."

Jjaks ran over to the wall and pounded back. "You shut the fuck up."

99

Freddie was climbing to her feet. She yelled, "Give me the keys to the car."

"No."

She held out her hand. "Give me the goddamn keys. Now."

"You want the fucking keys." He walked over to the top the dresser and picked them up. "You want them so bad, take 'em. You go drive out of here, that's okay by me."

She grabbed the keys out of his hand. "Yeah, I want to go. I'll find someone who can help me. You're so incapable, go out to get a few easy dollars and come back like this. I'll go out and do it myself. You can stay here, get drunk, and play with your goddamn ear."

There was a loud knock on the front door. "This is the manager. Open up."

Freddie said to Jjaks, "Just let me out of here."

He felt like holding her down, keep her from leaving. The manager knocked again. Freddie went to the door and opened it. The manager was a middle-aged man with a bowling-ball stomach. He took one look at Freddie and said, "You folks are gonna have to keep it down."

"Tell it to him." She pointed behind her at Jjaks. "See if he's sober enough to understand."

Jjaks said, "I'm sober." He tried to stand up straighter and fell against the bed, stubbing his toe and realizing that he was still holding the bottle of whiskey. He put it down on the floor and looked at the manager. "I'm not drunk."

"What happened to your ear?"

"What?" He felt like laughing. Behind the manager, Freddie was looking at him with contempt.

"God," she said, "you're pathetic."

He hiccuped. "Yeah. But am I drunk?"

The manager said, "I'm not kidding around here. Simmer down or I'll call the cops."

Jjaks felt his feet go out from under him, too drunk and in too much pain to stand up. He fell back on the bed, sat up, and said, "Yeah, call the cops. We love cops here." He looked at the door. "Freddie, you hear that? The man here, he's gonna call the cops and then go bowling."

Freddie said, "I'm outta here."

The manager said, "Bowling?"

"Your stomach," Jjaks returned.

Freddie said, "That's it."

Jjaks put his head down on the pillow. He looked blearily past the manager at Freddie. "You're leaving?"

"I need some air. I need to get out of this goddamn place. I'm leaving."

He said softly, "I'll let everyone know." He was too drunk to keep his eyes open.

From outside the room he heard a man's voice, the same guy who'd been banging on the wall earlier. "If you two don't shut up, I'm going to come over and make ya."

Jjaks heard Freddie yell back, "Get inside, you fat slob." And then she was gone.

The manager said to Jjaks, "I don't want to have to come back here." He walked to the door. "And I'm gonna charge you extra, bleeding all over my goddamn pillowcase."

Jjaks just lay there after the man closed the door. The room was spinning and he felt like he was going to throw up again. The last thing he remembered was the little black dog jumping up and licking his face.

Chapter 8

THERE WAS A BLOND waitress working in the diner that Sammy finally stopped in. Chewing gum, some tropical shade of lip gloss on her lips, she was wearing Reebok sneakers and little half socks that looked silly, but she had nice legs.

The diner was a tiny place. Stools and a counter on one side and a few tables on the other. There were bathrooms down a short corridor at the far end and a cash register next to the front door. The place smelled of stale cigarette smoke, burned coffee, and cockroach shit.

The waitress had a pad and a pencil in an apron pocket on her waist. She took one look at Sammy and said, "That your horse out there?"

Sammy had followed Jjaks two miles into the city, banging yellow lights and ignoring sounds from the trailer behind him. Twice, Sammy had lost him, but each time it was as if Jjaks got lost himself. He'd slow down, Sammy could see him looking at the street signs. When they finally stopped, Sammy felt like going over to the car and knocking on the window. He'd wait for Jjaks to roll it down and then tell him, You doubled back three times, you dumb fuck.

But he didn't. He waited until Jjaks went into a shitty little motel room and then he went across the street to the diner so he could see what was going to happen next.

The waitress had poured him coffee. Now she waved a hand in front of his face. "Hey . . ."

"What?" He could see their room from here and he had forgotten all about the horse trailer. It was parked outside.

He looked at the waitress. She seemed to be about nineteen, with blond hair turning dark at the roots and a nice body. She was wearing a pink skirt and blouse.

She asked again, "Is it? Your horse, I mean?"

"No."

"No? I thought I saw you pull in. That wasn't you?"

"I don't like horses." He looked across the street. Jjaks had gone in there ten minutes ago. Sammy was dying to know what was happening. Were they talking? Maybe Freddie was taking care of Jjaks' ear, treating him tenderly. She could be doing something else to him. Sammy didn't want to think about *that*.

The waitress said, " 'Cause, if it is your horse, you might want to know I think somebody's trying to steal it."

Sammy looked at the trailer. There were two drunks by the back of it. One of them had opened the rear door and the other was leading Clementine down the ramp. Clementine was an impressive animal, coal black, with a shiny blanket on her back and an intricately braided mane. Her nostrils were wide with excitement, or fear, and she stamped her feet a couple of times as the drunks maneuvered her.

One of the drunks got on top of her. She did a little dance across the street, but the drunk held on. He reached for his

103

buddy, helped him up on the horse, and they started to trot down the street, oblivious to the traffic.

The waitress said, "Well now, there's something I never saw before." She poured more coffee into Sammy's mug. "You see that? Somebody stole that horse. You sure it isn't yours?"

Sammy looked up at her and then out the window at Jjaks' room again. "Yeah, a horse thief. That's a hanging offense in this town, right?"

The waitress pushed the sugar container and napkin dispenser away, leaned down on her elbows, and stared directly at him. She had yellowish teeth, but that didn't bother Sammy. He thought they went well with her hair. She was grinning and it caused two dimples to appear, the one on the right slightly more prominent than the other.

A man came out of the motel office and went down to Jjaks' room. He pounded on the door, shouted something, and then pounded again. There was a dumpy-looking woman standing by the office door, the man's wife probably. It seemed unreal to Sammy because whoever it was seemed to be exerting a lot of energy, but there was no sound to accompany it. It was like watching a silent movie, an old Chaplin film.

The door to the room opened finally and Sammy drew in his breath. It was Freddie. Even from this far away he was amazed at how beautiful she was. He felt like an intruder, a voyeur, watching private activity from the shadows outside someone's bedroom.

Freddie was standing in the light from a street lamp and it highlighted her, made her seem larger than life. He wanted to run over there and take her in his arms, or kill her.

The manager leaned into the motel room, probably talking to Jjaks, and Freddie took another step into the street. She was looking down the road and Sammy realized she was watching the two drunks disappear on the horse. Then she looked directly across the street.

Sammy jumped over the counter and stood behind the waitress.

She said, "You can't do that." He had his hand on her shoulder and was moving her back and forth, keeping her in line with Freddie because he was sure she could see him.

The waitress said, "Cut it out. This isn't funny."

Freddie glanced away and Sammy let go of the waitress. He realized everyone in the place was staring at him. He shook his head. "Sorry, I thought I saw a ghost."

The waitress didn't seem that mad. She said, "I'll tell you what, I'll forget about it if you get back on your side of the counter."

"Sure." He was still watching Freddie. He dug in his pocket and came up with a few dollars, threw the money on the counter, and made his way over to the door of the diner just as the motel manager was coming out of Jjaks' room.

The waitress said, "Don't you want your coffee? You got a fresh cup here. On the house."

He didn't answer. Freddie was alone, walking down the street. Sammy knew he'd never have a better opportunity, so he bolted out the door and ran after her.

FREDDIE REACHED the car several yards ahead of him. As she was getting in he sprinted the rest of the way and slid into the passenger seat. She threw her hands up in surprise and gave a little yell. "What the fuck are you doing?"

"Is that any way to talk to your husband?"

"You're not my husband."

"Tell that to the justice of the peace."

"You didn't bring Red with you." She glanced behind him and Sammy realized she was afraid of Red. But not of him.

"Red?"

105

"He's not here, is he?"

"You don't have to worry about Red. You should worry about me. Red's not here anyway."

She sighed. "Good. In that case, get the fuck out of my car."

"No fucking way."

"Jesus, what do you want? Are you going to chase me around forever? I'm never coming back. I can tell you that right now."

"You're my wife."

"I am not. I don't care who you had perform the ceremony. I am *not* your wife." She opened the door on her side and tried to get out, but Sammy reached over and dragged her back in.

He said, "Look, I just want to talk to you. Get this thing straightened out. I think all it was . . . we got off on the wrong foot."

"Shit. Look, Sammy . . ." She had an edge to her voice now, a little confidence because it was only Sammy she had to deal with at the moment, not Red or Joe. "You think this is true love? Well, it isn't. I think you're a creep. I don't know what you thought would happen. I'd fall in love with you and we would live happily ever after? Is that what you figured?"

"All you got to do is give it a chance."

"A chance? That's a good one." She ran her hand through her hair, checking her face in the mirror. "Shit, I look like hell."

"I think you're beautiful."

"What am I supposed to do, fall into your arms?" She paused and seemed to be considering something. Then she gave Sammy her sweetest smile. "I'll tell you what. Let me have my money. Give me the cash and I'll make a deal with you. I'll give it some thought and we can get together in a day or so and see how things are."

Sammy laughed bitterly. "You need a little time to think it over? Is that it?"

"Sure. Time. That's all." She reached out and patted his knee. "Who knows, probably it'll all work out."

He reached behind his waist and pulled his pistol out. He held it loosely, almost as if he wasn't sure why he had it. It glimmered faintly in the light from the street and she could see it, against his thigh. He said softly, "I don't think so."

"What are you doing?"

"Don't worry about it. Just start the car up and drive."

"Where?" There was real fear in her voice suddenly.

"Just drive, I'll let you know."

She started the car and pulled out into the street. Drove slowly down past the motel and continued another quarter of a mile until they came to a little park. There were no other cars around and Sammy said, "Stop here."

"Look, Sammy . . . honey . . . maybe we did get off on the wrong foot. Hell, I'm adaptable. We get to know each other . . . who knows. But you don't need that gun."

Sammy looked around. The park was almost dark. He could make out a swing set on one side and a couple of see-saws. There was an asphalt track for jogging, but he couldn't see to the other end of it. Next to the swing set was a statue of some guy wearing a cavalry hat and sitting on a horse. It looked like pigeons had been shitting on him for a hundred years.

There was another statue, a riderless horse, a couple of feet away. Sammy thought it was supposed to be like the Tomb of the Unknown Soldier, until the fucking thing moved. It scared the hell out of him. It went from being absolutely motionless to taking a couple of steps toward the car and then prancing sideways.

He forgot about Freddie long enough to stare out the window. It was Clementine the Dancing Horse, minus the drunks. Eating grass calmly.

He reached into his pocket, pulled out the brochures, and showed them to Freddie. "Do you see what this is?"

"What?" She looked. "A house?"

"I bought this, a nice house. It's got a backyard, a fence. Wall-to-wall carpeting. We could be happy there. They got a pool and tennis courts right up the street. With the house, you got a full membership. It was gonna be a surprise, but I can tell you now."

"Sammy, I don't care about any house."

"Did I tell you this? I didn't just make a down payment, I bought the whole thing. You'd laugh if you knew what I had to do to get the money. And Red would shit his pants." He pointed at a picture in the brochure. "It's this model right here. Twenty-seven hundred square feet. Central air. Two-car garage and cable with, I don't know, a hundred and fifty goddamn channels."

Freddie said, "Listen, that's nice. A house, cable TV. You can watch movies all day long and have a great time. But right now I can't breathe. I have to get out of this car."

"Are you listening to me? I'm trying to tell you, we're talking a dream house here. A lot of people work their ass off all their lives, they never even get close to owning a place like this. I'm gonna buy a tractor. I'll go down to Sears and get one of those big goddamn mowers."

"Jesus, Sammy, you hear yourself? You want to cut the fucking grass, go ahead. But don't try to get me excited about it."

"It's the American dream." He was looking down at his lap, deep in thought. He could smell his own sweat and feel a warm wetness in his armpits. His heart was racing ahead of his brain, pounding in his chest as if it didn't know it had a limited number of beats and then was going to just quit someday. He still couldn't understand why she wasn't interested. A house like that. A beautiful place. Never have to work in a dive bar again in her life.

She reached for the door and he raised the gun. "*Don't . . .* open the door."

She let go and sank back in the seat. Sammy watched her for a minute. Her eyes were closed. She had a bead of sweat on her upper lip, her mouth was partially open, and she was breathing in quick gasps, like a dog might do on a hot summer day. Sammy thought it was sexy as hell. Breathing hard, either because she was hot or because he was scaring her. He thought about that. Scaring her. At least that was something.

He said, "Look . . . Freddie . . ."

She opened one eye and glanced in his direction.

"I know . . . Red said . . . your dream, you want more than anything to be a Las Vegas showgirl. It's what my momma wanted. It didn't work out for her, though. It's a hard life. Harder than you know. I saw what it did to my mother. But see"—he held the brochure up again—"you can have a wonderful life here. Live with me and we can make it work."

Suddenly a man appeared at the window of the car. A bum with a scraggly beard and only a couple of teeth. He pressed his face against the glass, peering in at them with wild eyes and an insane look on his face.

Sammy gave the bum a look, feeling stronger now because he knew Freddie was scared. He raised the pistol, let the drunk see it, and then watched the man stumble away. He turned back to Freddie.

"What do you say?"

"We'd be one happy family."

"Sure." He turned a page in the brochure. "You get to pick the carpet. They got"—he ran his finger down the print—"eggplant or ecru, whatever the fuck that is. You choose before you move in. Brand-new carpeting."

"Is that a color?"

"What?"

"Ecru. Is it a color?"

109

He glanced at the brochure. "I guess. Why else would they put it in?"

She acted like she had to think about it. "Since I don't know what that is, I'd have to pick eggplant."

For an instant Sammy thought she'd had a change of heart. He asked, "How many kids?"

"How many kids should we have? Is that what you want to know?"

He could see she was mocking him. He said woodenly, "Yeah."

"Geez, lemme think." She put her forefinger to her chin and pretended to concentrate. "Let's have, hmm, let's have two. A boy and a girl. A prince and a princess. How would that be? Is that what you want, Sammy, live in your dream house and have kids? You think it's as simple as that?"

"You're lying. You don't want any kids."

"Did I say that?"

He put his hand to his face, covered his eyes for a moment.

When he took his hand away, his expression had changed. Freddie must have seen the difference, because she said quickly, "Wait . . . wait . . . Sammy, I was only kidding."

He lifted the gun until it was pointed right at her head. She put a hand up, like she was going to shield the bullet if he decided to fire. "Sammy, come on. I was joking around. You want to talk about carpet, let's talk carpet. Eggplant . . . I like eggplant."

"All you want to do is treat me like shit."

"No . . . no. That's not all I want to do. I was upset. It's been a long night."

"You leave the wedding. You're my bride and you take off with my own brother." He seemed to be talking almost to himself, running down the list of things that had gone wrong. "I wanted to get you a nice house. Get you out of

110

those sleazy joints you dance in. And all I am is an asshole, a joke to you."

She reached out and tried to touch him on the knee, keeping her eyes on the pistol the whole time. "Sammy, that's not true."

"You really are nothing but a cheap slut, like your tattoo says. You like dancing naked, because that's all you'll ever be." He nodded his head vigorously. "You're a piece of trash and that's all you'll ever be."

Her voice was shaking with fear. "They made me get this tattoo. Everybody knows that. Red forced me. I'm not a slut. Listen . . . I'm upset, we're both upset. You don't need that gun. All we need is a little time. You put the pistol away. Why don't we go somewhere and have a drink?"

"Give me a fucking break. Go get a drink, me and you?"

"I'm serious. Listen, Sammy . . . you're a great guy."

"Right there, you're doing it again. Poor Sammy. Everybody treats me like dirt and now you're trying to be nice because you're scared shitless."

"I'm not scared. I just don't know, I mean, why would you feel like pointing a gun at me? We don't need a gun. Who needs a gun just to have a talk? Right? Why don't you put the pistol away?" Her hand was closer to his knee now, moving slowly.

He shook his head. "No, see, I already found out. People want to treat me like shit. They do it all the time. But if I got a gun, then they can't treat me like shit."

Her hand reached his knee and she stroked it gently. "Sammy, put the gun away."

"*Get your hand off me.*" He jerked back from her and started to squeeze the trigger. Saw her face turn white. She threw herself back against the car door and said, "Sammy, don't."

" 'Sammy, don't. Sammy, do this, do that.' God, I'm tired of this shit." He reached out and turned the radio on, turned the volume way up so he didn't have to think anymore. The

111

station was playing a song by R.E.M., "Everybody Hurts." He cranked the volume even further up until all you could hear was the music blasting against the closed windows of the car.

He screamed at her, "I'm tired of it. Tired of it all. You understand that? Does that get through your ears to your little fucking brain?" And then he pulled the trigger.

Chapter 9

HE DROVE FOR A while, trying to figure it out, what do you do with a dead body? He spent half the time crying, looking down at Freddie's corpse, sobbing his eyes out because he was sure he had really loved her. The rest of the time he talked to her, called her names, and said, "See, see that? That's what happens if you fuck with Sammy Clayton."

She lay limply, like a huge perfect doll, a goddess in death, except that there was a big spread of crimson on her shirt. At some point he reached over and turned her face away from him so she'd look like she was simply asleep.

He found himself back at Danny's 24-Hour Diner finally and realized that if he continued to drive aimlessly, he might get stopped by a cop. It would be a tiny bit difficult to explain. He decided the only thing to do was get rid of Freddie. He thought of his brother in the motel room. Figured all of this was Jjaks' fault anyway. Let him take the blame.

Matter of fact, since Jjaks and Freddie liked each other so much, Sammy could arrange a rendezvous.

The street was deserted, just a couple of parked cars and a few lights from the diner casting a dim glow on the sidewalk. The diner was open. Through the plate-glass windows he could see a couple of people inside, hunched over the counter. Other than that, there was no sign of life.

The brakes in his car squeaked a little, just outside of Jjaks' motel room. Sammy almost lost his nerve. He turned his car off and sat there scanning the parking lot and thinking of the waitress just across the street. The cute blond in the pink outfit. Maybe he could go across and get her to help him. They could drag Freddie's body somewhere and the waitress could tell Sammy how cute he was again. Then they could go back to the diner, get a cup of that terrible coffee. Drink enough of it and stay awake for days. Get to know each other.

He wished he had a drink. Something eighty proof. Didn't matter what it was, as long as it was strong. He had a gun. He had a dead body. A drink would help. Calm his nerves. Because the thing was, he was going to try to drag Freddie across the parking lot of the motel and get her inside Jjaks' room. That was the plan. He could get caught out here in the lot, or even if he made it to the room, who knew what was going to happen when he opened Jjaks' door? Jjaks was liable to be a bit angry about his ear.

A cop car came out of nowhere and Sammy almost pissed his pants. The patrol car moved slowly through the parking lot. Sammy couldn't decide, had someone called them? Was that what this was? The cops already knew what had happened, were aware that he was driving around with a corpse in his car, and were only waiting for him to make a move before they pounced?

He could imagine himself inside the city jail, that hell-hole down on Charles Street that he'd seen on television, Channel 11 news, and that he'd heard was worse than anything you could imagine. Him, alone, in there, for murdering some woman who'd done him wrong. He'd get torn to pieces.

He scrunched down as far as he could in the seat, watching the police from just over the dashboard and running several possibilities over in his head. Someone could have seen him shoot Freddie. Even that wino. He could have called the cops. Nah, no fucking way that geezer even had a quarter to make a call. Maybe just some stranger had called and told the cops what Sammy had in mind, what he was going to do with the body. But nobody knew what he was planning. There could be somebody right now, though, watching, but hiding. They'd seen Freddie's body somehow and Sammy, alive, behind the wheel. Figured Sammy had killed her, so they dimed him out. Dialed 911 and said, "If you all ain't too busy, you can catch yourself a murderer."

All this shit was making him paranoid.

There were two cops in the car, one driving and the other scanning the darker parts of the lot. Sammy could see the outline of their crew cuts as the car passed underneath the neon vacancy sign.

The car pulled close enough to Sammy's that he could see thin splats of dried mud on the fender well and a shiny new scratch on the hubcap that hadn't had time to rust yet. He heard the dry popcornlike sound of pebbles grating between the tires and the asphalt underneath, and the thin muffled cough of one of the officers clearing his throat. Then, for a second, all he could see was the reflection of the headlights on the car roof above him as he held his breath. He was sure that any second he'd hear a door close, someone was going to come rushing over, drag him out of the car, slam him up against a wall, and stick a big-assed Magnum in his face.

But it didn't happen like that. As suddenly as they had appeared, the headlights dimmed and the steady throb of the engine grew faint. Sammy inched his way up on the seat.

The police car was leaving. Brake lights came on like two cat's eyes and then winked out. The car pulled out onto the street and disappeared past the diner.

Jesus. Sammy let his breath out with a sigh and said out loud, "Goddamn, they're on patrol, that's all that was. A routine patrol."

Freddie had fallen sideways and was leaning slightly toward him. He couldn't see her face, just the lightness of her hair, and she appeared so natural, simply caught and frozen in the act of bending down in the seat, that Sammy almost expected her to straighten up. He felt an urge to talk some more. Give her a report on any further street activity.

He reached out tentatively, touching the top of her head. Her hair felt coarse and prickly against his skin, but he had the idea that it might be because he knew she was dead. He left his hand there for several seconds, the way you might if you were feeling something unusual for the first time, and then yanked it back when he realized what he was doing.

He leaned down until he could see the top of her face. She stared mutely at the vinyl surface of the upholstery. Her eyes were slits, puffed and lifeless. She gazed sightlessly at the floor of the car, a vacant expression on her face.

He had no choice. He couldn't leave Freddie in the car forever. Couldn't sit out here and wait for the cops to come back either. This time they'd remember his car, realize it had been there before. Might make them wonder. Plus, if he dumped her somewhere besides here, there would be a homicide investigation, and where were the police going to look first? At her husband, that was fucking where.

He gave it five minutes, to make sure that the police weren't coming back anytime soon, and then slipped out of his door and over to the passenger side of the car. It was harder than he thought, lifting Freddie out and onto his shoulders. She weighed a ton. Her limbs were loose and flopped awkwardly in his grasp. Every time he moved, she moved also, and it caused him to lose his balance. He stumbled and half fell out of the car, dragging Freddie out on top of him, so that they lay in some kind of obscene embrace. Her skirt had ridden up over her thighs and her arm had caught on the open window, swinging back and forth against the car as if she was using its momentum to lift herself above Sammy's pelvis.

He got to his feet somehow and heaved her onto his shoulders. Staggering, he made it across the parking lot. Just before he got to the door of Jjaks' motel room, he banged Freddie's head on the outside lamppost and said, "Jesus, Freddie, you okay?" before he remembered he was talking to a dead woman.

Now that the moment had arrived, he was unsure of what to do. He felt like smoothing her hair, fixing her makeup. He'd loved her, but he'd had to kill her. Everything was ruined and it was Jjaks' fault. Now Jjaks ought to take the blame, face up to it. Take responsibility.

It was only fair that Sammy march right into Jjaks' motel room like an adult and let him take the blame for it.

—◆—

SAMMY STOOD over his brother for three minutes without moving and watched him sleep. Jjaks was snoring with a peaceful expression on his face. Sammy remembered when they were kids. No matter what happened, Jjaks always looked like that when he slept. Not a care in the world. Sammy felt like reaching down and shoving his brother's face into the pillow, holding it there until Jjaks woke up. See who had worries then.

Sammy went around the room, wiping every place he could think of that he might have touched while carrying Freddie's body in.

There was a puppy on the bed. It had been asleep, pressed up against Jjaks' shoulder. As Sammy stood over Jjaks the puppy opened its eyes. When he stepped away from the bed, the puppy stood up, yawned, and wagged its tail. The dog followed him into the bathroom. He was tempted to kick the puppy. But if he did, it might make enough noise to wake Jjaks.

Sammy had thought, at first, coming in here and hearing Jjaks snoring, that Jjaks was simply asleep and might wake up any minute. But the door had slammed behind Sammy, catching him by surprise, causing him to think his heart was gonna stop, and Jjaks hadn't moved.

Sammy leaned down over Jjaks. Got a whiff of him. The man was passed out. There was an empty whiskey bottle on the floor next to him, a pint of Seagram's Seven Crown. It smelled like Jjaks had drunk the whole thing. Sammy relaxed. Now he could concentrate, get the job done.

He carried Freddie into the bathroom and arranged her carefully in the tub. While the water was running he went back into the room, got his bloody shirt that Jjaks had taken earlier, and hid the gun underneath the pillow. He had another gun at home and it would be easier, make more sense to the cops, if Jjaks had the murder weapon in the room.

He went back and looked at Freddie for the last time. She was beautiful, if you ignored the bloodstains on her side. He felt as if he ought to say something, some last words. His throat was dry and tight, though, and nothing came to mind.

The tub was halfway full, the water lapping at Freddie's stomach and thighs. She looked peaceful, more like she'd fallen asleep taking a hot, soothing bath than she'd been shot to death. He sat on the edge of the tub and thought, If she'd only given it a chance.

He reached down and touched her face. It felt warm, like the water. He figured she'd stiffen up overnight and the cops would have a hell of a time getting her out tomorrow morning. He spoke to her after all. "It doesn't matter, Freddie. They might have trouble getting you out of here. You might not look your best. But I loved you." He pointed into the other room. "Him? He doesn't know how to treat a woman. You'd have been better off with me. We could have made a nice home. You and me." He sighed. "It's better like this. This is how I'll remember you."

He turned the water off and left the bathroom. Pausing one more time to look at his unconscious brother, he sneered. "You. You should've stayed in jail. I don't care what they do to you. I don't care if you get the gas chamber. You deserve it."

He was halfway across the parking lot when he realized he still had the motel-room key in his hand. It made his head spin, making a mistake like that. He could picture the cops, finding the body and Jjaks sleeping it off. Sooner or later one of them would realize the key wasn't there. But then he figured there was no way he was going back into that room again.

Putting the key in his pocket, he told himself not to worry about it. Besides, what he'd like to do was watch the cops when they came to arrest Jjaks. Sammy wanted a front-row seat to see his brother's face when they dragged his ass out of that motel room and threw him in the back of a cop car. Jjaks wouldn't know what had hit him.

He walked to the diner across the street and picked up the pay phone.

―――

THE WAITRESS said, "You sure that wasn't your horse?"

"What?"

Sammy was sitting at the counter. He felt like shit, like he was gonna throw up. He'd called the cops to tell them about Freddie's body in Jjaks' room and no one had shown up yet. He could feel adrenaline pumping through his body, making him feel like he'd done speed for three days in a row and was getting ready to crash.

"That horse. It looked valuable to me."

Sammy remembered. "Clementine?"

"Was that its name?"

119

"Yeah. Clementine, the Dancing Horse. She was a show horse." Sammy was making it up as he went along. "I told you it wasn't mine? It was. I swear. A lot of people paid good money to see that horse dance. You wouldn't believe it— fox-trot, disco, you name it, Clementine knew the steps."

"You serious?"

"Sure."

"It could do all those dances?"

"Did I mention it could tango and carry a rose in its teeth?"

"You're joking."

"Huh?" Across the street a patrol car quietly pulled up and two officers got out. Sammy felt his pulse quicken. One of the officers was talking on a handheld radio and the other was walking over to the manager's office. Sammy felt his stomach lurch and had to put a hand over his mouth to keep from throwing up.

"Hey . . ." It was the waitress. "You don't mind me saying so, but you don't look good. You got a bad stomach?"

"You got . . . I don't know . . . you got a Coke? Something like that?"

"Sure."

He started to say something else when his stomach heaved. He almost threw up right there, but managed to get control long enough to gasp, "Where's the bathroom?"

The waitress pointed behind him and he bolted from the counter and made it to the men's room barely in time. He threw up, hugging the toilet and heaving until he thought his insides were going to come up. When he was done he staggered to his feet, walked over to the mirror, and cleaned his face.

He was freezing when he went back to the main part of the diner. Over the counter there was a display of sweat-shirts that said, DANNY'S FAMOUS 24-HOUR DINER—MINNESOTA on them. He said, "You know what? Gimme one of them."

"A *sweatshirt*? It's summer."

"I don't give a shit. I'm cold." He put the shirt on when she handed it to him and then turned to look out the window.

The cop had gotten the manager out of the office and was outside with him, pointing down at Jjaks' room. The manager was nodding, agreeing with whatever the cop said, and pointing too.

The waitress came back with the Coke and asked, "Did you call the cops?"

He felt like he'd gotten caught cheating on a test. "No . . . no. Why, did you?"

She said, "Well, somebody stole your horse."

He realized she was still talking about Clementine and not what was happening across the street.

She shrugged. "If I was you, I'd call the cops."

"No, listen to me, I didn't like that horse, okay? Two things about it. Number one, that horse was insured, and number two, it was a pain in the ass."

Suddenly something occurred to him. He hadn't forgotten Freddie was dead, but he also hadn't realized what it meant. It meant he had no wife. Jesus, he was a widower. He tried smiling at the waitress. Looking at her carefully because, for the first time in an hour or so, he remembered he was a single man. He said, "You wanna know something about that horse?"

"Sure."

"Everytime—and this is the truth—every time I see a good-looking woman . . ." He glanced outside. The cops and the manager were still there, huddled together. Another patrol car was slowly pulling up. Out of the corner of his eye, he saw a third appear at the end of the block.

He ran his hand through his hair. Made himself continue talking. "Anyway, say I go out somewhere, a show or something, and see a good-looking girl. Then Clementine, that's my horse, somehow or other she gets away. Every time. Last

121

time it was the trailer door. It broke and Clementine bolted. Took me two days to find her again."

"Yeah?"

"Honest." The expression on her face hadn't changed and he wondered if she even knew he was trying to flatter her.

She said, "So . . . ?"

"So what?"

"Come on. What about this time?"

"This time?" He smiled. He felt like Don Juan or maybe Don Johnson. One of them fuckers. Impressing the hell out of a woman. "Well . . . see, this time it was you."

She pushed his arm and laughed. "Oh, you're teasing me."

"You saw Clementine. She took one look at you and she ran. I swear to God, I think she gets jealous."

"She didn't run away. Those guys stole her."

He shrugged. "Same thing."

She stopped smiling and pointed past him. "I wonder what's going on over there?"

Sammy looked. The cops were banging on Jjaks' door. Any minute they were going to charge in and find Freddie in the bathtub. He'd sit there and watch. Then, since things were beginning to look up, maybe he would take this waitress out. Tell her some more horse stories.

He said, "Did you ever hear? They took two kids, scientists did. One kid was an optimist and the other kid was a natural-born pessimist. They put one, the pessimist, in a room full of brand-new toys, and the other kid, the optimist, they put him in a room full of horseshit. Came back an hour later and the kid with the toys was crying, told them all that's going to happen is the toys are gonna break, the batteries are gonna run out."

"Yeah?"

"So they went over to the other room, the one full of horseshit, and the kid had a big grin on his face, digging like

122

crazy, and they said, 'What are you doing?' And the kid smiles even more, keeps on digging, and tells them, 'All this shit, there's got to be a pony here somewhere.' "

"What's an optomist? That a guy who fixes your eyes?"

"What?"

" 'Cause I have to go see one. That story reminded me. I got to get my eyes checked."

He stared at her for a second. "Never mind."

Chapter 10

JJAKS MOVED ON THE bed and felt cold metal on his cheek, something digging into his face. At first he couldn't understand it. He had no idea where he was. He rolled over and tried to focus. The room was almost dark.

The side of his head was killing him, he knew that much. Tried to push himself off the bed and failed. *Goddamn*, his head was killing him. He reached up, touching whatever was gouging his face, and realized it was a pistol. He yanked his hand back. Even the idea of having a gun could get him into so much trouble.

He thought for a moment that he was back in the penitentiary. Christ, if they searched his cell and found a gun was fucking gone . . .

It started to come back, the motel room and Freddie. Fighting with his brother. He could feel a searing pain from his ear that helped to wake him up. He touched his ear gingerly, feeling queasy, and moaned, "Freddie . . ." Waiting for a response.

Outside, the sky seemed to be going crazy. There were red and blue lights flashing everywhere. He had to stop and think. Was it the Fourth of July? Was that the reflection of fireworks? No, he was fairly certain it wasn't. Besides, he would hear fireworks. So what was with the lights?

And what was with the gun? Although he couldn't figure it out, maybe it was Freddie's gun.

He tried calling her name again and came up empty. The sound of his voice seemed to bounce like a deadweight across the room.

He staggered to his feet and moved toward the bathroom. The lights outside were getting brighter. He could hear voices, muted sounds that seemed to carry a sense of urgency, but either he was too hungover and sick to understand them or they were too far away.

The puppy rubbed up against him, got caught in his legs, and Jjaks almost went over in a heap. He had to reach down, push the dog away, and tell it, "Pooch, what you're risking, you're playing with me throwing up all over you, so I'd keep my distance." The dog trotted ahead of him and lay down, whining, in the bathroom doorway.

Jjaks stumbled into the bathroom without turning on the light. He held his head under the sink for a long time, letting the cool water rush over his face. When he finished, he could still hear the puppy whimpering and the steady drip of the faucet leaking in the shower stall. He said through his hands, "You hungry, boy? You wanna eat? I'll get you something to eat, pooch."

In the mirror, his own reflection stared back at him grotesquely. There were bruises on his cheek that he must have gotten during the fight with Sammy, purplish blotches that redefined the texture of his face, gave it a doughy appearance. The entire side where his ear had been torn was swollen and inflamed. The ragged edges of his earlobe looked like it'd been through a food processor. Blood had crusted like dried strawberry preserves, hard and brittle.

When he touched it, it was much like running his finger along the surface of heavy-grit sandpaper, coarse and abrasive.

The dog kept whining. Jjaks realized it was probably hungry, maybe starving. He tried to find where it was by looking in the mirror. He knew it was close by, over by the door perhaps. He rubbed at the glass and could see the wall behind him, and below that, if he stood on his toes, the edge of the shower. No puppy there. The shower curtain was pushed a little to the side, and for the first time he saw a knee sticking above the rim.

It scared the hell out of him. "Jesus, Freddie, why didn't you say something? You scared the hell out of me just sitting there." He turned. "You know, we have to feed the pooch. Got to get some kind of food for him." The thought of going out was unbearable, with his head hurting this much, but if she was in the bathtub, he might have to.

He stepped over to the tub. "You asleep in there?" He pushed the curtain all the way over and then felt something in his stomach, the feeling he'd get if he won the lottery jackpot. But then couldn't find his ticket.

Freddie, beautiful Freddie, all banged up, with her head tilted sideways at a crazy, lifeless angle. Jesus, she was dead. What in the world had happened? What had he done?

He tried to remember, getting shaky images in his head like it was a bad dream that he was forgetting quickly now that he was awake. Flashes of the night before. He'd come home from Sammy's and done what? Drank that booze, for one thing. But maybe it was more than that, maybe he'd gone into shock from having his ear torn and the booze had hit him harder than he'd anticipated. It had to be.

He tried to think it through. Shit, they'd had a fight. He could picture pushing Freddie up against the wall, them screaming at each other, and the asshole from the next room banging on the wall. But Freddie had left. *Hadn't she?* She'd been standing by the front door, giving him a dirty

126

look, when the manager had come in. The manager had left, Jjaks knew that had happened, and so had Freddie. Hadn't she? Christ, he couldn't remember.

Had she come back later and they'd gotten in a bigger fight? Or she didn't leave and Jjaks had hit her too hard after the manager left? But if so, what the fuck was she doing in the bathtub? And what was he going to do now?

For a wild, hopeful second he thought she might've fallen in the tub and at least it wasn't *him* who'd hurt her. He clung to the hope that it wasn't his fault. But there was blood all over her shirt that hadn't been caused just by her falling. And where the fuck had the gun come from? It was sitting out there, right now, probably with his fingerprints all over it.

The phone rang in the other room just as Jjaks realized that he was truly a murderer. It was a sharp, strident noise that punctured the silence like a bomb going off. He listened to it, each ring seeming louder than the last, until he couldn't stand it anymore. He got up, stepped over the dog, walked into the other room, and picked up the receiver.

It was the manager of the motel, not even bothering to say hello, just blurting out, "Listen to me. I don't care what you got going in there, but I got a swarm of cops out here. They're about to break your door down, so you better get whatever it is cleaned up in there. I run a nice establishment. I can't afford this kind of shit."

Barely able to answer the man, Jjaks said, "What?" Confused. The man's words weren't sinking in. He could still see Freddie's knee in the bathroom. The pale white flesh from midthigh to the top of her calf seemed unreal to him from this angle, as if someone had molded a giant Barbie doll out of a lump of bone-colored clay and propped it in the bathtub. It looked like the backdrop for a television commerical. The camera would pass slowly over the shower and, at any moment, she'd move, leaning forward to tell the viewers what kind of shampoo she used. She'd ask him to bring her a clean towel.

The manager said, "I'm not kidding. I got enough worries without the cops coming here."

Jjaks sat up on the bed. "The cops? What the fuck you talking about, the cops?"

"I'm talking about the po-lice. They're about to knock the door to your room down and I'm trying to warn you. I don't want any trouble. And it's my goddamn door they're thinking of busting up."

Jjaks slammed the phone down and ran to the window. The *lights*, how dumb could he get? The lights he'd seen earlier, thinking it was the goddamn Fourth of July, were the police, out there in the parking lot getting ready to storm into his room. Not a big deal unless you stopped to consider what they'd do when they found a dead woman *and* the murder weapon right there. They'd probably shoot Jjaks on the spot, save the taxpayers' money.

He could hear rustling outside. Sounds that stuck out as having nothing to do with a normal night, the low murmur of disconnected and muted voices, the clunk of a car trunk being slammed shut and the soft tread of shoe soles on concrete. He imagined it was a SWAT team, wearing flak jackets and skintight leather shooting gloves, bristling with armor and resolve, positioning themselves for the final rush.

He had no idea what to do. What could he do? He had a dead woman in the bathroom, a hungry dog, and a wicked fucking headache.

⁓

THE COP was thirty-four years old but felt like he was sixty. He was due to go off shift in an hour and was suffering from a sour stomach and sore feet. His ass hurt from sitting in the squad car for most of eight hours, and his ears were stinging from listening to his partner talk almost nonstop for what seemed like the better part of a week.

128

The last thing he needed was some kind of bullshit domestic dispute, a lovers' quarrel in a pay-by-the-minute, no-tell motel. But somebody had called 911 and said there were weird things going on and he'd been sent to check it out. He wanted to call back to headquarters, ask them, You got a complaint that something weird is going on in *this* neighborhood? But they probably wouldn't get it.

His partner was on the other side of the door, with his hand on the butt of his service revolver. Behind them were two other units. He could hear them bullshitting quietly in the parking lot. If anything went down, they'd all be ready.

He banged on the door of Room 212 and stepped back. He heard a noise from inside, someone yelled something that he didn't quite catch. He banged again.

"Open up. Police." He looked at his partner, Don. Don nodded and said, "Hit it again."

Before the cop could, the door swung inward and a disheveled man with blood on the side of his face stepped out.

He was smiling. Looking from one cop to the other and saying, "Officers, what can I do for you?" in a tone of voice like he had something to hide.

The cop took one look at him, the way his face was fucked up and the way he moved rhythmically from one foot to another, and figured he was dirty. He glanced over the man's shoulder, tried to get a peek into the room. All he saw was the edge of a bed with the spread pushed down toward the floor and a small puppy at the man's feet.

JJAKS SAID, "How're you doing?" and then stepped to the side so the cop would see that he wasn't being sneaky here. There were two officers at the door and a couple more out in the parking lot that Jjaks could see. Jjaks was wondering if there was any way he could get them out of there without them having to come in the room.

He asked, "We having a problem?" Gave them his prison

129

look, the one he'd use if he was caught dead to rights by a guard and the man was trying to make up his mind what to do about it. Nothing challenging there, a blank look.

He had put a bandanna around his head to hide some of his wounds, but he knew he still looked like shit. His knees felt like they weren't going to hold his weight. He had trouble focusing, kept looking from one cop to the other, expecting at any minute they were going to pull out their guns and start shooting at him.

Jjaks made himself relax. Leaned against the door frame as nonchalantly as possible and pasted a big smile on his face. It made his ear hurt even more and he wasn't sure how long he could keep it up.

The puppy whined and stepped through Jjaks' legs. He reached down and picked it up. Petting the animal, he said, "Is this what it's all about? The puppy? The manager complain? Listen, if it's a problem, I'll take care of it. My wife and I . . ." He lowered his voice. "It's her dog. We aren't going to stay much longer. Just through tomorrow. So, I mean, if you fellows could look the other way?"

One of the cops asked him, "What took you so long to answer?" He was a big man, with a belly that stretched the fabric of his uniform pants but large muscles underneath the fat. No expression on his face and a hard edge to his voice. There were handcuffs on his belt in a little leather pouch, a nightstick that banged against his leg when he moved, and the polished leather handle of a blackjack sticking out of his hip pocket. Jjaks could picture him beating the shit out of a prisoner, taking that lead-weighted sap out in one fluid motion and cracking the side of someone's head with it.

The other cop was younger. He had a thin whisker line along his chin and the faint outline of a mustache above his lip. His hair was cut marine-corps short and seemed almost white against the lights from the parking lot. He was staring at Jjaks without saying a word.

Jjaks said, "I'm sorry, I was in the bathroom and my wife is asleep."

The cop said, "Your wife inside?"

Jjaks looked him right in the eye. "Yes."

"Well, we had a complaint."

Jjaks nodded, gave it a quick second, and then asked, "A complaint?" Like he was too stupid to see the connection.

"Yeah. Yelling. Somebody called it in."

"I had the TV on, you think maybe it was that?" He took a step outside the room, blocking the cop from getting more of a look behind him. "Listen, Officer, it's been a bad day. My wife isn't feeling well and she was yelling a little bit. You know, blowing off some steam."

"But she's inside now?"

"Yeah."

The other cop asked, "What happened to your ear?"

The first cop said, "Let me talk to your wife."

Jjaks said, "My ear?"

"What happened to it?"

The first one said, "We have to talk to your wife. See her for ourselves."

"She's asleep." He turned and grinned at the second cop. "I got in a fight. My stupid brother and I . . . he bit it off. We were fighting." He spread his hands. "It was stupid. Very stupid."

"Yeah?"

Jjaks laughed. "But I got him better."

The first cop said, "Your wife . . ."

Jjaks shook his head. "I told you, she's got the flu or something. She just now fell asleep. I don't want to wake her."

"I have to take a look."

Jjaks seemed to be considering it. He stepped aside finally and said, "All right, Officer, I know you got your duty. But please, can you be quiet? Christ, we had a hell of a time earlier. She felt terrible." He held his finger to his lips. "You think we can do it quietly?"

The cop said, "I just want to make sure everything's okay." He stepped past Jjaks into the room. It crossed Jjaks' mind that if he was going to run, if he was to have the slightest chance of taking off and trying to get out of town, this was the last best time he'd ever get. But his legs didn't feel like they would hold up if he tried to run. Instead, he smiled one more time at the second cop, said, "You know how people get when they're sick," and turned to follow the first cop into the room.

THE COP was standing next to the bureau. Inside the little motel room he looked even bigger. When he was joined by Jjaks and the second cop, the room seemed to shrink, as if they would have trouble even turning around.

There was a small light on the bed table, casting a yellowish glow on the bottom third of the wall, and a cone of brightness on the ceiling above. They could see, over in the double bed, the blanket-covered figure of Freddie. She was on her side, with the covers pulled up around her neck and her face turned away from the light. She appeared to be sleeping.

Jjaks gestured at the bed and whispered, "See, we're all right. I was just a little worried because she had such a high fever. We only got married today. This is our honeymoon. Wouldn't you know it, here I am, in a motel with my new wife, and she's as sick as a dog."

The cops were starting to lose interest, or so it seemed to Jjaks. He was thinking, Get them headed toward the door, get them out of here. He didn't even want to look at Freddie because it seemed to him that every time he did, the cops did too. Sooner or later they were bound to notice she wasn't sleeping.

He made himself look one more time and was getting ready to ask the cops if they'd seen enough when he noticed there was a spot on the sheet. At first he couldn't figure it

132

out, what the hell was it? But he realized, Jesus Christ, even as he was looking it was getting bigger. A bright, dark stain, like fresh red paint, flowing outward in a circle that was already as big as a silver dollar, spreading onto the sheet by Freddie's torso even as the two cops were standing less than ten feet away.

The first cop must've seen something in Jjaks' face because he asked, "What's the matter? You're sweating."

Jjaks did the first thing that popped into his head. Glancing past the cop, he yelled, "Hey, don't do that," at the puppy sitting calmly in the middle of the room. He quickly walked over to the dog and picked him up.

"He gets that look on his face and the next thing you know he's pooping on the floor. I got to get him out." Jjaks could still see Freddie, but the cops had turned away and were watching him and the dog. "You mind, Officers? I got to walk the dog." While he was talking he was moving toward the bed, keeping his body between Freddie and the cops. He got to the bed, still holding the puppy, and leaned down, afraid to move but knowing he had to do *something* about the spreading blood.

He forced himself to ignore the police behind him and to lean down, putting his lips on Freddie's forehead. He kissed her softly and said, "You sleep well, baby." Then, leaning even closer and pretending to listen, he said, "No . . . no . . ." loudly enough for the cops to hear. "It's the police. That's all. Everything's all right." As he straightened back up he scrunched the blanket up so that it hid the bloodstain.

The second cop was looking at him hard. Jjaks thought they were going to insist that he wake Freddie up. The cop said, "You been in trouble before?"

Jjaks thought about lying, but if he did and they checked, he'd be in even more shit. So he gave them his con look, defeated, and mumbled, "Yes, Officer. But things are different now. I got my wife—" He pointed toward the bed and immediately regretted it. "See, I'm trying to make a go of it. That's all." He felt like screaming at them, yelling that they should leave, get the fuck out of there because he didn't know how much more he'd be able to stand.

The cop leaned back against the door frame and asked, "You do time?"

Jjaks nodded. "A little."

"What for?" The cop's gun butt was resting against the bureau. There was a piece of something a couple inches away from the gun butt, some greasy-looking hunk on the floor that Jjaks realized with horror was the missing piece of his ear.

Jjaks cleared his throat. "I stole a car . . . a couple of cars." He made himself go over toward the cop. "Look, I really am trying to go straight. You fellas want to talk to me. I can understand that. But can we move outside? I don't want to wake my wife."

The two cops looked at each other and Jjaks could almost hear them thinking. Finally the first cop shrugged and said, "I think we've seen enough. You take care of your face, tell your wife we hope she feels better."

The second cop added, "No more fighting. We have to come back here and we're gonna lock your ass up, I don't care if your wife is so sick she's dead. We'll still take you downtown."

"Absolutely, Officers. Don't you worry. There won't be another peep out of this room."

"Make sure there isn't."

After they left, Jjaks stood in the center of the room. Blood was rushing through his head and he felt like his heart was gonna come through his chest, it was beating that hard. He sank down slowly on the floor with the puppy in his lap. The puppy wagged its tail and then hopped up onto the bed.

Jjaks didn't know what to do. What was he going to do with Freddie, for one thing? Where was he going to go?

He stepped to the bed and sat down. He pushed the covers away from him, over toward Freddie's body, and to his horror they were pushed back. He leaped to his feet, stared at the corpse, and whispered, "Freddie . . . ?" But then he saw the black paws of the little dog. It was nestled between the pillow and Freddie's body, playing. Jjaks picked it up and set it on the floor. He sat down on the bed again and tried to think.

One way or another, he had to come up with a plan.

⁓

SAMMY COULDN'T believe what he was seeing. The cops were actually leaving Jjaks' motel room? What the fuck was going on? He felt like running over and shouting at them, Hey, jerk-offs, what are you doing? There's a dead woman in that room. He saw Jjaks leaning in the doorway, watching the police depart. How had Jjaks pulled it off?

He wanted to call the police back and say, Wait a minute, you need to go back in there and look around. But what good would that do? All it would accomplish would be to make the cops wonder who was it that was watching the motel and making these phone calls? Shit, they might come after *him*.

Behind him somebody said, "Must've been a false alarm." He realized that the waitress had been standing there the whole time, watching the same thing he had been. Sammy hoped he hadn't said anything out loud.

He nodded. "I guess."

And then Sammy had an idea. If Jjaks had pulled it off, fooled the cops somehow, well, he still had a body in there and he had to get it out. He couldn't leave Freddie's body there, because somebody would find it and the cops already knew Jjaks had rented the room. They'd catch him in minutes if he did that. No, Jjaks had to make a move. Had to get Freddie out of there one way or another. All Sammy needed to do was wait.

He turned to the waitress. "You know what? I think I'll have another cup of your coffee. I might be here awhile."

She grinned at him. "You gonna go the whole route, cream and sugar too?"

He winked. "Ain't no need for sugar when you're around, right?"

THE FIRST thing Jjaks did, after the police had left, was put the puppy out in the car. Then he cleaned up every bit of mess in the room. He wiped the blood off the floor where his ear had been, cleaned the bathroom, and tore the sheets and pillowcases off the bed. He took them out to the car too and then went back and spent a long time looking at Freddie's body.

Jjaks said, "You got to understand, Freddie. I don't have a choice. I'd like to give you a decent burial, you know, at a church, get a nice headstone and all that. But I can't."

He went out and pulled his car up as close as he could to the room. Making sure first that there was no one around, he dragged Freddie out as quickly as possible and put her body in the trunk. Then Jjaks ran around, started the car, and was out of there without seeing anyone.

Chapter
11

IT CROSSED JJAKS' MIND, Minnesota, Land of Ten Thousand Lakes. It was written on every license plate. He could tie a bunch of weights to the body and heave it in one of those lakes. Hell, drive all the way up Interstate 35, dump the body in Lake Superior. No one would ever find her.

But the thought of Freddie swaying underwater, tied to some kind of anchor, was more than he could bear. The only thing to do was to give her a decent burial.

He drove slowly out of town, headed north, up toward White Bear Lake on Highway 61. There was an old campground there that he knew, back in the woods. He figured he'd find a nice quiet spot and bury Freddie.

He turned onto Route 244, following it around the southern side of White Bear Lake, past Birchwood. The houses started to disappear behind him. Here, there were lodgepole pine trees, acres of deserted countryside, and a dark, open sky, sprinkled with millions of stars as if someone had opened a can of silver glitter and hurled it up toward the clouds.

It was dark enough that Jjaks had to turn his high beams on and lean closer to the windshield. The white lines in the middle of the road seemed to come whipping up at him, like lances shot from a huge catapult just ahead of him.

He followed the road until he could turn off, get into a wooded area just past the old campsite, where no one was likely to be. The road ran parallel to the shore and then veered away, cutting through some tree-covered hills on one side and a ravine on the other. Below him was Gem Lake, much smaller than White Bear, with Gibbs Island in the center of it, a small dark smudge of land from this far away. To get to the water you'd have to walk a couple of hundred yards down the ravine and then through a thick growth of saplings. It was perfect.

He pulled off the road. It was eerie. He could hear frogs from the edge of the water, deep-throated burping noises that seemed to echo back and forth along the bank of the lake as the frogs answered one another, and the high-pitched, loony sound of some kind of bird calling from the woods. Above him and over to the left, between the lakes, were the falls. He could hear the muted roar of water running over rocks as it traveled between the two lakes. Heat lightning played in the sky high over his head, like some giant camera flash illuminating everything for one instant and then plunging the earth into darkness the next.

The ground was hard and dry. His shoes scuffed through the dirt as he walked around the car and opened the trunk. He grabbed the body the wrong way at first, upside down, and got confused in the darkness. It was horrible, seeing flashes of Freddie's face from the lightning, as if it was one of those silent films from years ago, everything jerky and out of context. One minute she'd appear before him, her head tilted sideways and a slack, lifeless expression on her face, and then he'd not be able to see her at all.

The wind picked up and it began to spook him. The sound of the trees rustling was like an audience, a witness to this terrible deed he was about to perform.

He got his arms around her waist finally and dragged her from the car. The route he took toward the woods was tortuous, a meandering path through and around small thickets of bushes made worse by the fact that he was dragging the body backward and couldn't see half the time. At last, he just gave up and laid her on the ground.

He sat down beside Freddie, straightening her arms and legs. "Freddie . . ." His voice cracked. "Jesus, Freddie, I'm sorry. I'm sorry." He began to cry, falling to his hands and knees and pawing at the earth frantically while tears ran down his face.

It was nearly impossible to dig. He found that all he could do, with his bare hands, was scrape at the dirt. He walked back to the car finally and got the jack and used it like a shovel, but even then it was slow going.

"Jesus, Freddie, I can't even give you a decent burial." It wasn't working. There was nothing he could do except leave her there in the shallow depression and cover her up as best he could.

He laid her out like a queen, his very own Cleopatra, moving her body tenderly into her grave, wrapping her arms across her chest and smoothing the locks of her hair again at the sides of her face and away from her forehead. He pushed what little dirt there was over her body and then went into the woods, tore a branch from a pine tree, and covered her face.

He stood looking at the grave for a long time, wishing he had never come back or that he had met Freddie a long time ago, before his life had become complicated. He wished a lot of things, standing in the quiet backwoods. He realized that if things had been different, it would be a nice place to have a picnic. He thought about that, about bringing Freddie down there with a wicker basket full of fried chicken and fresh-baked bread. They could've spread a blanket on the ground, eaten, and then made love under the sky. He wondered what his life would have been like if things had been different, if his mother hadn't abandoned him and his brother hadn't been such a shit?

He could picture it almost, like something just beyond his reach—him and Freddie, happy. He realized, miserably, that the one chance to make things right in his life might just have been snatched from his grasp. And all he had was himself to blame.

———

SAMMY WATCHED it all. He parked above Jjaks and watched his brother carry the body into the woods. It was hard to see; Sammy had to squint into the darkness and look off to the side slightly, not stare directly at Jjaks. He could see Jjaks' shadowy figure most of the time but twice lost track of what Jjaks was doing and where he was.

When he saw Jjaks lay the body on the ground and start digging, he whistled softly to himself and murmured, "Jjaks, old buddy, you're cold, you know that? Goddamn, bringing her out here. And I bet you don't want anybody to know either. Am I right?" He chuckled softly. His brother was going to go to a lot of trouble here. He wanted to tell him not to bother. He could ask him, What's the point? Jjaks, you want to look at it like this. It ain't like it's gonna be your little secret. But it was a lot of fun seeing him work this hard.

He'd followed Jjaks from the motel, wondering where the fuck was the man going? Was he thinking of driving to Canada, for Christ sake, take Freddie to the northern tundra and bury her there?

Sammy still had no idea what Jjaks had done to convince the cops to leave, but that didn't mean shit now. He *had* Jjaks and that was a fact. He thought of the expression *dead to rights*, and it made him grin into the darkness. He had Freddie dead, and now he just as likely had Jjaks dead. The

140

man was going to wind up in that little green room over at the state penitentiary, and somebody was going to drop a capsule into a cup, let Jjaks breath fire for a while. Jjaks could come out here and try to bury the body, dig with his bare hands, and think he was getting rid of evidence. It didn't matter. One way or another, Jjaks was a man on death row. A dead man walking.

~~~~

THE WOODS became quiet minutes after Jjaks left. Now that only Freddie was in the area, it was as if nature settled down, took a deep breath, and paused for a few moments. The bird out by the lake stopped calling. The shadows still moved across the trees and there was an occasional flash of heat lightning, but it didn't show up as brilliantly because the whole sky was lighter. Wind blew softly across the thin covering of dirt where Freddie lay buried. A gentle breeze. That's all it was. It was cool and seemed to bring with it a quiet animal murmur like a baby waking, a yawn and then a sigh.

There was silence and then the stirring again, this time stronger, accompanied by pain, and slowly the dirt stirred. First one side, like a miniature earthquake, and then the other. Suddenly one of Freddie's hands poked through the soil and her fingers twitched spasmodically. Her other hand followed, and in an instant they were clawing clumsily at the branch over her face.

It felt like she was awakening from a deep sleep. She'd had her tonsils out when she was a child and it was a similar sensation, as if coming through a long tunnel, fighting the effect of the anesthetic to consciousness. She was aware of a throbbing pain in her head, worse than any hangover she'd ever experienced, and the same stiff, bruised feeling to her limbs that she'd have if she rolled down a steep, rocky hill with her hands tied behind her back.

There were vague memories now of her last hours in the

motel room. She thought perhaps she'd seen Sammy but couldn't imagine when. How she'd ended up here, half-buried under sticks and loose earth, was a complete mystery.

She heard a car cough into life about a hundred yards away and struggled to sit up. It took all of her strength, but when she did she saw the taillights of a car. It was a red Camaro, the one Jjaks and she had taken from the front of Nora Clayton's house on her wedding day. Jesus, had that just happened the day before? It felt like twenty years ago.

She called, "Jjaks?" Her voice sounded weak and far away to her ears. The soft meowing of a newborn kitten. The car was moving and she began to crawl toward it, slowly at first but then more frantically as the car gathered speed. She tried again, yelling, "*Jjjaaaaaaakkkkkss* . . ." but the car kept going. By the time she got to the highway, on her hands and knees, there was no sign of it. It had to be a mile away by then.

Freddie lay on the ground, bruised and bleeding, not even lifting her head as a big semi went roaring past with its horn blasting. She didn't even know the semi had stopped until she felt strong hands lifting her.

—⁄⁄⁄⁄—

SAMMY CLAYTON stopped at the first pay phone he saw and called the cops. He drummed his fingers impatiently on the glass of the booth and practically shouted into the receiver when it was answered.

"Listen, I saw it, the whole thing. Jjaks Clayton, he stole his brother's car and he killed that girl, Freddie. Yeah, I'm not fooling here. You better pick him up and you'd better send an ambulance out to 393 Landover Street. You got a lieutenant out there, Lieutenant Ben Costikyan. He knows who I am. I already talked to him earlier. Jjaks Clayton beat the shit out of him. You better go check it out. And remember, Clayton is an ex-con." He hung up the phone.

142

JJAKS WAS driving west. He didn't know where he was heading and didn't care. What difference did it make? Everything would be better if he just got as far away as possible. He still couldn't remember exactly what had happened, how Freddie had died, but he was afraid that when he *did* remember, he was going to feel even worse.

He saw a light through the office window of a small used-car lot and stopped to pay cash for a beat-up twelve-year-old Chevy Malibu. The guy that sold it to him picked up the phone as Jjaks was walking out. Jjaks didn't know who he was calling, but he didn't care either. He got on Interstate 694 and was simply going to follow it as far west as he could, get out of the state, and then decide where he was going to end up.

Just where the interstate passed the exit for Vadnais Heights, he saw the first cop car. It was stopped at the exit ramp. As Jjaks went whipping past he saw the cop watching him, saw the blank stare of authority, and wondered if the policeman was going to pull him over and hassle him. It occurred to him that there might be some kind of APB out on him. Maybe the guy back at the car lot had called the cops. Just because of the way Jjaks looked or because of the gas station or, shit, who knew, maybe someone knew about Freddie.

The cop started out after him but didn't turn his lights on. A quarter of a mile farther down, Jjaks saw two more cop cars. He had enough time to check in the rearview mirror, see that the first one was still there, when its overhead lights went on and he heard the wail of a siren. He glanced at the puppy in the passenger seat. Its tongue was hanging lazily out of his mouth and it was panting contentedly, its tail making quick, brushing sounds on the seat. Jjaks said, "Fuck it, huh, pooch? Fuck it. They want me, they can fucking try to catch me." He stomped on the accelerator and the Malibu shot forward.

143

Ahead of him one of the cop cars turned sideways to block the road, but Jjaks managed to wrench the wheel to the right and slide past. There was a tearing scrape of metal on metal and Jjaks felt a jolt go through the Malibu. But then he was free.

He started to laugh out loud, feeling life in his veins for the first time since he'd discovered Freddie in the bathtub. Here's how it would end, in a fiery crash after a car chase. He could see it, pictures in the papers tomorrow. MAN ELUDES POLICE BUT THEN DIES. It was fitting.

He went around a bend and there were two more cop cars ahead of him, one coming directly at him and the other, off to the side, about to enter the highway. Jjaks rolled down his window and yelled at the top of his lungs, "Come on, you son of a bitch. Come and get me."

He careened off the side of the one cop car, had the satisfaction of seeing a shit-scared look on the driver's face, and then he raced toward the car ahead, swerving toward it on purpose. The cop behind the wheel veered away, but Jjaks kept after him.

He screamed, "You fucking chicken," and laughed insanely. He could remember the game his brother had played with him. Sammy had grabbed his hand and held it on the burner. Playing chicken.

He was furious all of a sudden, mad at the world. These fuckers wanted to treat him like this, chase him down. That was fine. He never meant to hurt anyone. Never had an honest chance in his life. If this was how it was going to end, then he wasn't going alone. He'd take some sorry motherfucker with him.

It was a terrific feeling, beating the cops at their own game. He came up to a rise in the road fast enough that his wheels left the ground and then slammed back down to earth with a jolt. The second he hit the ground, after he'd gotten control of the car, he peered through the windshield and got a glimpse of five cop cars together, lined up one by one across the road. There were at least a dozen heavily armed policeman, waiting. They weren't that far ahead and Jjaks had no idea whether he could stop even if he wanted to.

But he did, at the last possible second, out of instinct. He slammed his foot down on the brake pedal and went into a long, screeching skid. He had time to watch the expressions on the cops' faces as he approached, holding on to the steering wheel tightly, like it was the controls of a 747 and he was about to crash-land.

He stopped ten feet from the nearest police car. His own automobile stalled. He sat there, looking at all the guns pointed directly at him, and reached idly out to pet the dog. He was tempted to get out and run, let them gun him down and be done with it. He never got the chance. The door next to his left shoulder opened violently and a huge black man in motorcycle boots, a police helmet, and a leather jacket grabbed him, pulled him out, and threw him on the ground.

Another cop—Jjaks couldn't see more than his shoes—started to read him his rights. He listened for a few seconds, heard the man say, "You have the right to an attorney . . ." and decided, Fuck it, no sense listening to that shit.

He could hear the man's voice droning on but didn't care. The night was over. His life was over. They'd check him out, discover he was an ex-con, probably find out what kind of night he'd had. Then he'd spend the rest of his life in jail or die in the gas chamber.

Right now, lying on the ground while some big-assed cop knelt on his back, he wasn't sure. Was that such a bad deal? He lifted his head to look at the man's shoes one more time and then settled back to the pavement in defeat.

~~~

THEY SEARCHED Jjaks again when they got to the station. Then they put him in a room by himself and went around

145

to an adjacent room to watch through one-way glass. At least that's what Jjaks figured they were doing. He had to fight down an urge to get up and make faces in the mirror. He didn't give a shit, would it make them mad, but it crossed his mind that somebody might come in and beat the fuck out him if he pissed them off too much more.

They let him sit there for over an hour, trying to make him sweat, and then Ben Costikyan came in and sat down opposite Jjaks.

Costikyan looked like shit. He had a bandage above one eye and his other eye and cheekbone were puffed and purpled with bruises. Jjaks had the idea he wanted to beat him to death. Have Jjaks on his knees sobbing out a confession in the first five minutes. He was moving in that careful way someone did when they had a cracked rib or two. The only thing he had in his hands was a folder with Jjaks' arrest report in it. He opened it and started to fill in some of the blanks.

Jjaks sat there quietly for about half a minute and then said, "They got you up late, huh, Lieutenant? All this fuss, what'd I do, exceed the speed limit? I could save you the time, let you go home to your wife and kids. All you have to do is tell me how much the fine is." He took a deep breath and then asked, "You seen my puppy, by the way?"

Without even looking up, the man said, "Shut the fuck up, asshole. No-fucking-body talks to me like that."

Jjaks leaned forward. "The car's not stolen. I bought it."

This time the lieutenant did glance at him. "I'll tell you what, you piece of shit. I got a headache that no amount of extra-strength anything is going to take care of. You want to give me shit, act like nothing is happening here, we can all go out to the back lot and rearrest you. This time there'll be more of a struggle. Somebody might get hurt. You know what I'm saying?" He looked at Jjaks like he couldn't stand the sight of him. "Boy, you are in a world of trouble."

Jjaks said, "Look . . ." but it was all he could say. His

146

thoughts were swirling. What was he supposed to do, try to outstare the man? Demand a lawyer? He wasn't sure he knew any lawyers.

The lieutenant took a picture out of the folder, an eight-by-ten, and stared at it. Then he slid it across the table to Jjaks, upside down.

"Tell me her name."

Jjaks asked, "What?"

"Look at the goddamn picture and give me a name."

Jjaks picked the photo up. The picture was slightly out of focus. When they'd blown it up, it had gotten a little blurry. But it wasn't a problem telling who it was.

He said, "Lieutenant, we both know who she is."

The lieutenant yelled at him, "You prick. I have a headache the size of this fucking room. I also got what you might call a personal interest in this 'cause it just so happens I liked that girl. I am not having a good night. What might make my headache go away is the thought of putting your sorry ass in jail."

Jjaks finally said, "You know I know her, if that's what you want to know." He looked at the photo again. "She's . . . she's my brother's wife."

The lieutenant sat down. "Freddie?" he asked, as if he'd never seen her before. "How long have you known her?"

"I've known her . . ." He hesitated. "I met her yesterday. For the first time."

"You've known her for a day?"

Jjaks shrugged. "Look, are you going to tell me what this is all about? A lot of people know her."

"What's her last name?"

"What?"

"Her last name, what is it?"

"Clayton. I mean, that's what it is now. She's married to Sammy. My brother."

"I know who the fuck Sammy is. I didn't ask you that. I asked you what her last name is. Tell me *that*."

It shocked the hell out of Jjaks because he realized that he'd never known. Jesus, he *fucked* her and he didn't even know her last name. He said, "I'm not sure."

The lieutenant walked around the table, looking at Jjaks the entire time. "I got information that this beautiful girl was murdered last night."

Jjaks tried to look shocked. "What?"

"Shit boy, I'm not talking English, is that it? I tell you a fact and you look like you can't understand me."

Jjaks said, "Look, I barely knew the girl."

"That's not what I heard. I heard you two were *real* close. You want me to believe somebody else killed her, just because a lot of people knew her?"

"I didn't do it."

Now the lieutenant walked over to Jjaks, leaned over his shoulder to touch the picture of Freddie, and said, "All those people who knew her . . . how many of them . . . besides you, that is . . . how many of them have been fucking her for the last twenty-four hours? You got any idea what the answer to that might be?"

Jjaks said, "Shit." It just popped out. He looked at the photograph and then up at the lieutenant and asked, "What's going on?"

"What's goin' on? I'll tell you what's going on. Somebody killed that little girl last night. I can feel it in my gut. And I have information about where her body is buried. You want to know who gave me that information? Hell, boy, I'll tell you. It was your own brother. Your own brother dimed you out and he's waiting right on the other side of that wall to take us out to where you buried the body. *That's* what's going on." He sat back down in his chair. "You want to know something else?"

"What?"

"I know you killed her."

Jjaks mumbled something and the lieutenant glared at him. "Is that a yes or a no? It doesn't matter to me. Your

148

brother, Sam, says he knows where you stashed the body, and if that's true, it's a sad thing. Freddie was a beautiful girl with her life ahead of her."

Jjaks felt like crawling into a hole. He shook his head slowly and whispered, "No."

Costikyan said, "I'm going to prove it, you son of a bitch. I liked that girl."

Kicking the chair aside, he stood up quickly, grabbed Jjaks, and buried his fist in Jjaks' stomach. Jjaks collapsed heavily on the ground, having trouble catching his breath.

The lieutenant looked down at him and grinned. "What happened to your ear, Jjaks? The little lady bite it off in the struggle?"

"Fuck you. It fell off one morning. I woke up and there it was on my pillow. Strangest thing."

Costikyan kicked him twice in the gut. "You know what? I think my headache is starting to go away. What do you say we get together with your brother, have a family reunion? Take a drive and see if we can't find where you buried that poor girl." He squatted down next to Jjaks so his knee was pressing into Jjaks' gut. Jjaks could smell his breath, stale, with a tinge of garlic and booze.

"That sound like a fine idea to you, Jjaks?"

Chapter 12

SAMMY SAID, "UP HERE, go around the lake just a bit and then pull off. Another hundred yards is all."

He was in the front seat of Costikyan's car, excited and talking fast. Jjaks was in the back with Detective Lloyd Gold.

Jjaks, if he had the chance, would've clawed his way through the seat to get his hands on his brother. Sammy was having a hell of a good time taking the cops to Freddie's grave. Jjaks thought somebody ought to smack the shit out of him.

"This is the spot. Right here. I saw him carry her into the woods." He smirked. "Thought you'd get away with it, Jjaks?"

The lieutenant glanced in the rearview mirror and caught Jjaks' eye. "We'll be there soon, Jjaks. What kind of fucking name is that anyway?"

Sammy said, "It's what was written on his birth certificate. It was supposed to be Jack, but they spelled it wrong."

"Is that what it is, a typo? You a typo, Jjaks? A stupid fuck-ing typo. That's all your life amounts to."

Jjaks said to his brother, "Sammy, I don't know why you're doing this. You know I didn't kill anybody. When I get out of here, I might kill you, though."

Costikyan laughed and said to Detective Gold, "You hear that, Lloyd? We got a prisoner, I'm already planning to charge him with murder, and now he's making terroristic threats."

Sammy said, "Stupid son of a bitch."

Jjaks turned and stared out the window. It was only a mat-ter of time anyway if Sammy really did know where he'd buried Freddie, and it certainly seemed like he did. It had to be, because he'd followed him somehow and watched it happen. There was no other way to explain it. So what good was it going to do to bitch about it? In another couple of minutes they'd find Freddie's body and the rest would be history.

Costikyan pulled the car onto the shoulder of the road when Sammy told him to. Sammy hopped out of the car, with a look on his face like a five-year-old kid about to go on an Easter-egg hunt, and ran ahead. Jjaks got out more slowly, followed by Detective Gold. Jjaks could hear Sammy up ahead, crashing through the brush, his voice coming back like some phantom announcement, "Lieu-tenant, over here. It's right over here someplace."

Jjaks thought maybe he'd just wait there until they brought Freddie's body back out. He didn't know how it would happen; did they get the medical examiner, the coro-ner, whatever, up here to make sure she was dead and then carry her out on a stretcher? He wasn't looking forward to seeing her again. Not like that.

The air felt cooler, almost clammy, and Jjaks wished he had a jacket. There was a breeze blowing in from the lake, and the idea that they were here to uncover a dead woman from a grave she'd lain in less then a few hours gave Jjaks the chills.

It occurred to him that one thing he could do was confess. March right up to Costikyan and say, All right, you got me. I may not remember all of it, but I do know you're going to find Freddie up there in the little clearing under an inch and a half of dirt.

The only thing was, he couldn't do that in front of Sammy, couldn't give him the satisfaction. Sammy wanted to dime him out, that was one thing. But Jjaks wasn't going down on his knees in front of Sammy.

He felt the breeze pick up, tugging at his collar like unseen fingers, and he let his breath out carefully, trying to slow his heart. Detective Gold stepped around the car, took Jjaks' handcuffed arm, and started to lead him toward the sound of Sammy's voice.

Costikyan was up ahead, between Jjaks and Sammy. Lloyd Gold took three steps with Jjaks and they both stepped into the overhanging branch of a tree. Gold swore and said, "It's darker than hell out here."

Costikyan looked back and laughed. "That's right, Lloyd. And guess what? Jjaks baby is gonna find out for sure. We find this girl's body and old Jjaks will wind up in the gas chamber. Go straight to hell. He can send us a postcard from there, let us know if it looks like this place. Maybe a little hotter, though, right, Jjaks?"

Detective Lloyd ignored Costikyan. He pushed Jjaks and said, "Come on, Clayton, we may as well get this over with."

They walked another fifty yards and came upon Sammy. He was staring at the ground with a look of intense concentration on his face. The beam of Costikyan's flashlight exaggerated his features, making him seem grotesque. The bruises that had formed from Jjaks pummeling his face gave him a deathly appearance, as if he was the one who had been buried. Costikyan played his flashlight over Sammy's face and said, "You look like a fucking corpse, you know that?"

Sammy wasn't listening, he was walking back and forth, mumbling to himself.

The lieutenant said, "Well . . ."

"Give me a minute. It was dark when I was watching him. I know she's right here someplace."

"We don't got all night, so hurry it up."

Jjaks didn't get it. It wasn't that dark out here, not with the two detectives shining their lights all over the place. Sammy was right. It *was* right here, the grave. The place where he'd put Freddie's body. It was right here. Except, it wasn't.

He wondered. Was it possible that both he and Sammy were wrong? That they'd confused the spot with some other place along the road? Someplace closer to the lake that looked like this area? Was there another clearing like this one, where Freddie's body was lying, even now, undisturbed? He started to hope and then realized that with daylight coming soon, they'd have people out looking all over for her by midmorning.

Detective Lloyd asked Sammy, "Sure this is the right spot?"

"I'm sure. It was right here."

"There's nothing here."

"Don't point out the obvious, Lloyd," Costikyan told him.

Jjaks was barely paying attention. His eyes were riveted to the ground, staring at a hollow uncovering of topsoil and an area of brush that was strewn unlike the surrounding earth. It *was* the grave, or at least what remained of it. This was the spot, absolutely, but Freddie was gone.

He blinked his eyes hard because it crossed his mind, with all that he'd been through, perhaps he was hallucinating. When he opened his, though, nothing had changed. Sammy was still walking in circles, searching in vain. Lieutenant Costikyan was watching him and getting impatient. Detective Lloyd was watching Costikyan.

No one was paying attention to Jjaks. He stepped over to the burial spot and scuffed his shoes through the dirt so the impression wouldn't be so obvious. Then he said, "Lieutenant," indignant, "I don't know what you think you're gonna find, but it isn't here. My brother's making the whole thing up. I didn't kill anyone and I certainly didn't bury anyone out here." He looked directly at Sammy. "Matter of fact, I've never been here before in my life."

"The hell you haven't," Sammy yelled. "I saw you."

"Where's the fucking body, Sammy?" The lieutenant was getting pissed.

Jjaks said, "There isn't a body." He turned to Detective Gold. "There never was a body. I tried to tell you guys, the woman split. She got mad at me and left. No big deal. For all I know, she's in another part of the state. Who knows with women like that."

He had no idea what had happened or where Freddie's body had gotten to. All he knew was that it was lucky for him that she was gone. He stepped up to Costikyan. "You drag me downtown, interrogate me, all on the say-so of my brother, who, we all know, is a liar. It's obvious he's trying to frame me for something that never even happened. So, if you don't mind, I'd like a ride back into town."

Costikyan gave him a dirty look. "You'd like a ride back into town?"

"Uh-huh."

The lieutenant turned to Sammy. "How 'bout you? You want a lift?"

"Look, Lieutenant, I swear to Christ I ain't bullshitting. I saw the whole thing."

"Yeah?"

"I swear."

"Fuck you. Fuck you for dragging my ass out here in the middle of the night to go on some kind of wild-goose chase.

154

You think I got time to fool around? I'm a cop, people depend on me. I don't have the time to fuck around with a couple of losers like the two of you. You guys want a lift back to town? You're sure as hell not getting one with me. You can walk." He took a step closer to Sammy and shoved him to the ground. Sammy put his hands up instinctively and Jjaks thought for a minute that Costikyan was going to hit him.

"Lieutenant, this is the spot," Sammy insisted. "I *know* it is."

Costikyan had a wicked grin on his face. "Sammy, I can't blame you. If my wife's name was tattooed on half the dicks in town, I'd wish she was dead too."

"Lieutenant, I don't think—" Lloyd Gold began.

"That's right, Lloyd, you don't think. Right now you aren't getting paid for thinking. You're getting paid to do what I say. And I say that both these assholes are going to spend the rest of the night walking the fuck out of here." He looked at Sammy. "Unless you want me to drag you back, charge you with giving false evidence, somethin' like that?"

After a few seconds of silence Costikyan nodded. "I thought so. Enjoy your nature walk. You comin', Lloyd, or do you want a little exercise yourself?"

━━

SAMMY STARTED walking along the highway, ahead of Jjaks. He kept up the pace for a few minutes and then let Jjaks catch up to him. Jjaks was too tired to play games. When he caught up to Sammy, he didn't say anything. They trudged along for a while and then Sammy said, "I saw you do it, you know. I watched. Followed you out there and watched you bury Freddie."

"You didn't see shit."

"I just don't know how you did it. How you moved her body."

"What body? The one you couldn't find?" Jjaks was silent

155

for a moment, listening to Sammy breathing heavily because he was out of shape. There was sweat rolling down the side of Sammy's face. Jjaks figured this was the most exercise his brother had gotten in a long time.

It wasn't quite dawn yet, but Jjaks was able to make out the shadowy outlines of trees against the sky. There was a faint tinge of lighter gray on the horizon, and just a hint of orange. He pictured the sun as a big, brilliant helium balloon, sitting just below his line of sight, ready to pop out any minute.

He said, "Sammy, you wanna know what it was like, the first time?"

"Huh?"

"The first time. With Freddie. What do you think I'm talking about? I'm talking, the first time I banged your wife. You want me to tell you what it was like? It was fucking awesome. That's what it was like." He stopped walking and pulled his shirt up to reveal a purple mark on his stomach. "She bit me. Got so carried away that she *bit* me. Think of that. Tell you the truth, I didn't even feel it." He laughed. "I guess I had other things on my mind."

"Fuck you."

"That's what Freddie said."

Sammy glared at him and then jogged ahead about twenty feet. He stopped as a car came up behind them, turned, and stuck out his thumb. The car whizzed by. Jjaks shouted, "You really think someone's going to stop for you, you prick?"

"As long as they don't think I'm with you, they might."

"Right."

Sammy stopped walking, waiting for Jjaks to get closer again, and then said, "Gimme a cigarette."

"I ain't giving you a goddamn thing."

"Come on. Gimme a cigarette. I know you got some."

Jjaks reached into his pocket, pulled his pack out, and handed a smoke to Sammy. Sammy stood there expectantly. Jjaks ignored him until finally Sammy said, "What about a light?"

Jjaks grinned. "You got your cigarette. Get your own fucking light."

"You fucked my wife. You killed my wife. And now you won't even give me a match. Jesus."

Jjaks could now see in the dawn sky that it was a beautiful spot, a clearing surrounded by towering trees. Up ahead, there was a steep hill on the other side of the road, dotted with lodgepole pine trees, oaks, and an occasional cedar tree. Below them, in the distance, he could see another lake. The morning sun reflected off the surface of the water, a mirror image of the sky, complete with pink-tinged clouds.

Jjaks took a deep breath. The air smelled wonderful. He wasn't used to it, being in prison and then at his mother's house. Wasn't used to being outside and breathing air that didn't smell like old cooking or the sweat from a thousand other men.

He took his time about replying. "You know what, Sammy? I didn't kill Freddie. I'll tell you, at first, waking up in the motel room and finding her, I thought maybe I did. But now I know I didn't. I might've fucked her. That was the good part. But kill her? No way. I can feel it in my bones. I didn't have anything to do with that. I think I know who did, though."

Sammy looked away. "Who?"

Jjaks stared at him for a long time. "The second time, the second time I fucked her, I believe that was even better. In your own car. She had her legs wrapped around me and we damn near got killed. I'll tell you what, she knew how to fuck."

Sammy swore and took a wild swing, which Jjaks ducked easily.

Jjaks said, "You wanna know something, you piece of shit. All those years ago, you thought it was funny to hold my hand on that stove. You think it was funny tonight to try to get the cops to bust me for murder? Who the fuck is laughing now?" He didn't feel like laughing at all, but he wanted to see Sammy upset.

Sammy tried to hit him once more and Jjaks again dodged just as easily. He pushed Sammy playfully on the forehead, almost slapping him, and said, "Come on, big brother, is that as good as you can do?"

Sammy feinted and Jjaks fell for it. Sammy poked a weak jab towards Jjaks' face. As Jjaks moved away Sammy kicked him in the crotch. Jjaks felt his insides roll up and die. Thought he was gonna puke but managed to stay on his feet. Through clenched teeth he said, "I'm gonna kick your miserable ass, motherfucker." He made himself swallow the pain and danced back to Sammy with his fists raised.

He said, "You knew, everybody knew, she didn't like you. It was no secret that she was marrying you just because Red had some kind of hold over her. And people knew you let them tattoo her arm. They cut her with a knife, you bastard. Wrote *slut* on her arm. That make you feel good, Sammy?"

"I didn't tell them to do it."

"Who did?"

"I don't know. Red maybe. Jesus, she was my wife. I loved her."

"Bullshit. You didn't love her. And the only reason she was your wife was because she had to marry you." He danced in close to Sammy, faked a punch to Sammy's ribs, and then hit him hard on the mouth. Sammy went down. Jjaks stood over him and said, "You know what I think? I don't think I killed her. I think it was you who killed her."

"No."

"Oh, yeah, I think so."

"So where's the body, then?"

Jjaks laughed. Sammy was trying to get back to his feet.

Jjaks let him do it and then said, "Back there, with the cops, you knew. You were ready to tell them exactly where she was."

"I saw you put her there, that's why."

"You were setting me up."

"I think you're setting me up."

Jjaks was dead tired. He didn't know what had happened to Freddie and he was almost beyond caring. All he wanted was to find a bed somewhere and collapse. Sleep for ten days and maybe, just maybe, when he woke up things would be better.

He said, "Lemme tell you something, Sammy. If I was setting you up, if I cared enough to, which I don't, I sure as fuck would do a better job of it than you did."

He would have said more, but a pickup truck was rolling past. It slid to a stop. Some kid, teenager with freckles and red hair, giving them the once-over, probably thinking he couldn't wait to be a bad-assed dude like these guys, leaned out. "You fellas need a ride?"

They raced to the truck, both of them scrambling into the bed from different sides. Sammy clawed at Jjaks' legs, tried to push him over. Jjaks elbowed him out of the way.

The kid frowned at them. "You know, I got to think there's room for the both of you."

They drove off toward the sun. Jjaks and Sammy sitting with their backs against the cab, watching the place where Freddie had been buried get farther and farther away, not saying a word.

⎯⎯

THE KID drove them all the way back to the city and then dropped them off at the Dew Drop Inn on Warren Road so Sammy could get a shot and a beer with breakfast. Jjaks didn't feel that good, hungover and beat-up. Besides, since he'd gotten out of prison, he hadn't been eating real well.

He sat there, watched Sammy do his shot, and lost any appetite he might have come in with.

Sammy wiped his mouth, took a swallow of beer, and said, "You know what? You look green. You getting ready to puke?"

"How can you do that this early in the morning?"

"This? Hell, this is easy, it keeps me going. I come here all the time. All you need to do is practice. That's all."

"Shit."

Sammy leaned forward. "I'll tell you what."

Jjaks had to move back because he could smell the whiskey on Sammy's breath.

"You get a hangover, I mean, it's killing you. . . ." He picked up the shot glass. "Instant cure."

Jjaks told him, "All you're doing is making it last, making it so that when you go get hungover, it's worse."

"Bullshit." Sammy put his elbows on the bar and called down to the bartender. "Billy?"

The old guy ambled over. "Yeah?"

Sammy put a five-dollar bill on the bar. "I want to show this boy somethin'. I don't like him at all; matter of fact we hate each other. But he thinks he's a big man and I wanna see him take an early-morning drink. You get your best bar whiskey up here and pour me a shot." He winked at Jjaks while Billy poured the drink.

Jjaks said, "No way I'm drinking that thing. Not this early."

"Hold on." Sammy looked at Billy and said, "I'll tell you what, you pour just a little bit, like five drops. Pour a little bit of crème de menthe in there. Make it easy on the boy." He told Jjaks, "Tell yourself it's mouthwash."

"Forget it."

"Chicken?"

"Cut the shit, Sammy."

"Buck . . . buck . . . buck." Sammy was mimicking a chicken.

Jjaks laughed. "Jesus, you're stuck being a motherfucking kid, you know that?"

"You don't got the balls, just like you didn't have the balls to touch that stove."

"Is that why you had to hold my hand there? Had to help me?" He held his hand in the air so they'd both see the scar. Then Jjaks picked up the shot glass. "This comes back up, I'm aiming it at you."

The whiskey didn't burn as badly as he thought it would. He could taste it, but only for a second and then the crème de menthe coated his throat. It sat there for a couple of seconds, in his belly, like it was making up its mind, and then settled.

Sammy was grinning at him. Jjaks said, "You son of a bitch."

"Didn't I tell you?"

"Whew." Jjaks shook his head and glanced at the bartender. "Hey, Billy, two more."

Jjaks sipped at the second one. Digging in a pocket, he pulled out a cigarette, tossed it into the air, and tried to catch it in his lips. It missed his head completely and landed on the floor behind him. He dug in the pack and put another one in his mouth carefully.

He turned to Sammy. "Why'd you do it?"

"Do what?"

"You gonna tell me or not? What happened, you have a fight? You and Freddie?"

"I'm not talking about it."

Jjaks was starting to feel the whiskey. "Sammy, you know I know. Why fuck around with it?"

"Maybe it was somebody she met. She might have gone outside last night, after you passed out, met some guy and brought him back to the motel." He had a bitter look on his face. "She was so quick to hop in the sack with you, maybe she went looking for someone else."

161

"You think so? Let me ask you this. How do you know I passed out last night?"

"Lucky guess, that's all."

"A lucky guess?"

"Yeah. And I'll tell you something else. I'm not letting you out of my sight."

Chapter
13

THEY WENT TO SAMMY'S house finally. The place was a mess, with piles of newspaper stacked haphazardly around the living room and a thick coating of dust on every surface. A stale odor of fried food was strong in the air. It was hard to see because the only light in the room came from a single bulb in the ceiling. Jjaks looked up at it and asked Sammy, "What'd you do, you spring for a forty-watt? Trying to cut costs?"

Sammy said, "What?" and Jjaks shook his head, never mind.

The shades in the windows were up, but the glass was so dirty that not much light was getting through. Some things from the wedding, Sammy's tux and a couple of unopened bottles of cold duck, were strewn on a couch that, originally, had been white but now was yellowed with age and God knew what else.

Jjaks picked up a newspaper, spread it on the couch, pushed aside the cold duck and the tux, and sat down.

Sammy flicked the remote at the TV and they sat there, with an old episode of *The Honeymooners* on. Jackie Gleason was giving Art Carney a load of shit because his sewer work clothes had won the Halloween costume competition. Jjaks and Sammy slowly fell asleep in the dimness of the overhead light and the bluish glow from the TV.

Jjaks was dreaming when the sound of the telephone ringing yanked him back to consciousness. He had no idea how much time had passed. It took some time just to find the phone. He had to follow the ringing into another room and dig through a pile of dirty laundry on the dining-room table before he could grab the receiver. Sammy, awake now too, yelled out, "Don't answer it."

Jjaks ignored him and picked it up. "Hello."

A voice on the other end, a man, said, "I saw you. You and that brother of yours."

Jjaks had heard the voice somewhere, but he couldn't place it. "Who is this?" He could feel his hand gripping the phone, hard, the tendons in his wrist stretched tight. He had to tell himself to relax. See what was happening here and then decide whether or not to get anxious.

"I manage the motel. You know who I am. I saw you. After the cops left. And before that. First one of you carried her in and then the other carried her out."

Jjaks said, "I guess you got the wrong number, pal. Or this is a prank. You got my number and called up, trying to be funny."

"Don't hang up. If you hang up, if you don't want to hear what I got to say, then I guess maybe the police will listen."

From behind Jjaks, Sammy asked, "Who is it?"

Jjaks covered the phone. "Shut the fuck up."

The caller was saying, "You there?"

"I'm here."

"Well, Mr. Clayton. My wife and I both saw it. Made us sick. One of you carrying that woman . . . her body . . . into the room and the other carrying it out. Oh Lord, that poor

164

woman." He cleared his throat. "I think you know what I'm saying here."

"I think I do. What do you want, you thinking of flying first class to Hawaii? Got your eye on a new car? Is that what we're talking about here?"

"I'll tell you what. Fifty thousand oughta do it."

"I think you do have the wrong number. You must think you're talking to a guy with a lot of money."

"Listen, I don't want to be hard about it, you got your own problems. But I don't want to bullshit around either. I know you can come up with that kind of money. And I gotta have it by this afternoon . . . or I'll have to go to the police. Do my ci-vic duty."

"You're a good citizen, huh?"

"I try to be, 'cept I can understand, in this case, what's done is done. Best get on with business."

"And all this is, this is business?"

"I'm trying to get by, just like everybody."

"Okay. I gotta discuss this with someone. You can under-stand that."

"Sure, just don't take too long, okay? I want to know in an hour. And don't come looking for me. You won't be able to find me."

"How do I get in touch with you?"

The man chuckled. "Nice try. I'll get in touch with you. I'll call you in an hour. Don't disappoint me. Don't disap-point yourself, Mr. Clayton."

Jjaks said, "No, I won't. Do me a favor?"

"What?"

"I'm giving the phone to my brother. You tell him what you just told me."

"Wait."

"Yeah?"

"One more thing. If you've got it in your head to find me and kill me, I'll tell you something. I sent my wife away. She knows who you are, knows what you did. Anything happens to me, if I don't call her by a certain time, she goes to the cops. Understand?"

"I'll keep it in mind."

He handed the phone to Sammy, said, "Guy wants to chat with you," and watched the color drain from his brother's face. After a few minutes Sammy hung up, looking away from Jjaks.

Jjaks said, "You hear what he said?"

"What are we gonna do?"

"The man . . . on the phone . . . did you hear what he said? He said . . . one of us carried her body into the room and . . . one of us carried her out. I only carried her out. . . . I mean, I couldn't remember. You bastard, you let me think it was me."

"Look . . . it doesn't matter." Sammy sounded scared. "It really doesn't matter who killed her, right? It's the two of us, he saw me, and he saw you. My life is in your hands. Your life is in mine. That's the way it's supposed to be, right? Blood is thicker than water and all that shit."

"It matters! I loved her. You killed her, you fuck. It matters." Jjaks shook his head despairingly. "Aw, Freddie." He looked at Sammy. "It's always something with you, first this"—he shoved his burned hand in Sam's face—"and now this." Jjaks' anger exploded and he threw himself at Sammy in a violent rage, trying to choke the life out of him. He screamed, "Why'd you do it? Why'd you do it, why'd you do it?"

Sam yelled, "Get off me, get off me, you're killing me."

"Listen to me, you asshole," Jjaks said, " 'cause this is what's gonna happen. You buried me in this shit and you're gonna dig me out. You're gonna give me the money."

"What money?"

"I'm gonna go and pay that motel guy off."

"Please, there is no money."

"Yes, there is, it's stashed everywhere. Freddie told me, you lying sack of shit."

166

"I don't have it anymore, it's gone. I bought a house, half a house, near Vegas, for me and Freddie. Almost half a house."

Jjaks let go of Sammy, but continued to glare at him as he asked, "A house? You bought a house? What're we gonna do with a fuckin' house? Hey, you have to get that money."

Sam said, "Wait . . . wait, I got it. This is what we do. We go to where you hid her body. We get rid of it once and for all. Make sure they don't find her in a thousand years. Then we don't have to pay nobody nothing. See?"

"You're an idiot."

"What?"

Jjaks said, "I never moved her body. Goddammit, poor Freddie."

He shoved Sammy into the wall, hard. "We were *there*. It was right where we were. I never moved her body. It was just gone. You really think I had time to go back and dig her up?"

"What do you mean, you didn't move her body? You *had* to. You're fucking with me. You moved her. She didn't get up and walk away. Don't lie to me."

"You ate my goddamn ear off, you framed me, and now you're upset 'cause you think I'm lying to you? Jesus." He picked Sammy up off the couch by the collar of his shirt and shoved him against the wall. From three inches away he said, "Listen to me. If you fuck this up and I go to jail, I swear to God, you're going too. And I've been there before, I can handle it. If those boys see your white ass coming into the prison gates, though, they'll be lining up to get a piece of you. You understand what I'm saying? Either you do this right or I'll take you all the way down with me."

"What are you gonna do?"

"I'll go calm the motel guy down. He says I won't be able to find him, but I'll bet he's calling from his office. I'm going to talk to him. Tell him that you're coming with the money."

Sammy shook his head frantically. "But I don't have the money."

"Get it."

"How?"

"The same way you got the money for your dumb fucking house. Go down to your boss. I don't care whether you got to beg, borrow, or steal it. You just get it. Then come down to the motel office. We'll get this straightened out."

"Red won't give me the money."

"You figure out a way to get it. That's all. Bear his fucking children if you have to. Just do it." He walked to the front door. "I'll meet you at the motel in an hour and a half. That should be plenty of time."

Sammy said, "Hold on." He walked over to a bureau and opened a drawer. When he turned, he had two pistols in his hands. He held one out to Jjaks. "Take this. Just in case."

"I don't need a gun."

"Just take it. What if this guy decides to fuck us over?"

"You don't get it, Sammy. I ain't here to hurt anyone. I never wanted to hurt anyone. All I want is to settle this thing and get the fuck away from you and everybody else in this shitty town."

—⁂—

A HALF an hour later Sammy was in the alley behind Red's pinball arcade. There were two ways to get into the arcade. You could enter off the street, Planter Avenue, or you could go in through the back door by the garbage cans, where the rats and roaches hung out.

The block was deserted, so when a cat jumped out behind some trash cans and rubbed across his leg, it scared the shit out of him. He kicked at the cat and snarled, "Fuck off." He made himself take a couple of deep breaths and then peered in the back window of the arcade.

He could see endless rows of video games. It was like looking inside a huge spaceship. He felt like Captain Kirk

168

at the controls of the *Enterprise*. All those lights, some of them blinking on and off, it looked like science fiction. He moved to another window farther down the alley. Had to drag a box over and stand on it to see inside. He peeked in. Red was sitting at his desk, counting money. Sammy grinned. Red was counting slowly, like he didn't do too well with numbers, licking his fingers every couple of seconds and laboriously laying the bills, one at a time, out in stacks on the desk in front of him. To Sammy it was a sign from God.

Red had spent the better part of the last five years pushing him around. Treating him like shit and making fun of him. Even the wedding, with Sammy thinking that Freddie was wonderful, had been a joke. He remembered Joe, the thug who worked for Red, lifting the hem of Freddie's dress like she was a piece of meat. And Red laughing when Sammy complained.

Well, fuck that. And fuck Jjaks too. Jjaks thought that all Sammy could do was screw things up? He'd show him differently. He'd show them all. He was gonna go in there and demand some money from Red.

As he put the key in the lock it made a noise like a skeleton rattling. The sound bounced off of the building across the street and seemed louder than hell to Sammy's ears. He walked past the silent arcade machines until he got to the door of Red's office. He considered knocking, it was what he always did, but then decided, the hell with that. The new Sammy didn't knock for anyone.

Instead, he pushed the door open, seeing a startled look come over Red's face as he did so.

Red calmed down just as quickly, losing the surprised look on his face after just a couple of seconds. He was holding a stack of bills in his hand, but put them down as he said, "Well, look what the cat dragged in. I was just thinking about you."

Sammy wanted to do something positive, forceful. He

169

felt like kicking a chair over or pulling out his gun and waving it in Red's face. But already he was losing his nerve. Red looked huge and mean sitting there behind the desk. He certainly wasn't acting like Sammy was of any concern. Wasn't acting the least bit nervous, which Sammy would have preferred.

Red said, "I was planning to go looking for you, but you saved me the trouble."

"I did?" He could hear a tremor in his voice and it pissed him off.

"Yeah. You and me, we got to have a talk."

"I don't know. Maybe I should come back later. You look busy."

Red spread his hands over his desk. "You mean *this*?" He pointed at the money. "Nah, this can wait. All I'm doing here is counting my money. I'm not as good at it as you, you know, I don't have your head for figures. But I thought I'd give it a try. Count my own money for a change, instead of leaving it up to you. I'm finished. But I got to tell you, all this adding and subtracting shit is hard, very hard. I don't pay you enough, maybe."

"Well . . ."

Red said, "Why don't you sit down?" He pointed at the one other chair in the room. "Sit." Like he was talking to a dog. "Tell me why you came to see me." He laughed. "There's got to be a reason I'm blessed by your presence. Right?"

"It can wait."

Red's voice changed to a low growl. "No, Sammy, that's the thing. It can't wait."

Sammy nodded. "Well, okay then. See . . ." He didn't know where to begin but finally decided to plunge right in and get it over with. Red was scaring him. He'd seen it before, where Red would be dealing with somebody who'd made him mad. He'd start out being polite, but then all hell would break loose.

170

Sammy wished he hadn't come. He said, "See . . . I'm in kind of a bind, you know? I wanted to see about . . . to see . . . I wanted to borrow some money, maybe." He finished lamely. "I don't know."

Red grinned. "Sammy, your coming here now, you got more balls than I thought. You want money? Is that what you're telling me?"

"Uh, sure. Just a loan."

Sammy decided the best way to play it was to act like a jerk. Not a hard thing to do, because just talking to Red, seeing the man was a little annoyed, and Sammy not knowing why, was making his knees shake. But that's what Red would expect. Sammy to be a wimp.

Sammy took his wallet out of his pocket, opened it up, and laid it on the desk. He tried grinning, getting a squirrelly look on his face, and said, "Red, you see what I'm talking about? I don't got a thing in my wallet. Not a thing."

He left the wallet where it was and pulled the rest of his pockets out. "That's it. I got an empty wallet. Must not be my day, huh? So, you know, what with me being married now and all . . ."

"You want more money?"

"Sure. I could use a little bit, see me through, help me with this house thing." Sammy was saying whatever came to his mind. He couldn't get any feeling about what was going on behind Red's eyes. The man seemed almost too calm about it.

"*More* money."

"What?"

Red stood up. There was not a pleasant line in his face. "That's what I said. I said, *more* money. You prick, you come here, you got the fucking balls to ask me for money. You think I don't know what the fuck you've been up to?"

"Red . . ." Sammy had shrunk back in his chair. "I don't know what you're talking about."

"How's your new house, you fucking crook? You think

I'm adding this shit up for my health? You've been ripping me off for months now. I got you a fucking job, I pay you well. Hell, I even got your wife for you. And this is how you repay me?"

"I didn't take nothing. I swear, Red."

"Bullshit." He picked Sammy's wallet up off the desk. "You hand me this crap, show me this and act like you're broke. You're like a little fucking kid, Sammy." He dropped the wallet, came around from behind the desk, picked Sammy up, and threw him against the wall. While Sammy was down Red reached behind his desk and pulled out a baseball bat. He said, "This thing is thirty-two inches long and I'm gonna bust your head open with it." He held it over his head while Sammy scrambled on the floor.

"I want it all back. I'm gonna break your legs anyway, but then you're gonna give it all back to me. Every last dime and every last seed of every joint that you smoked that didn't belong to you."

"Red, I don't have it anymore." He could see the words *Louisville Slugger* written plainly on the bat and he was scared to death, seeing it in Red's hands and knowing the man was going to start hitting him with it any second. He remembered reading, somewhere, a story about Al Capone. The man had killed two of his own men with a baseball bat. If Red had heard the same story, it would be the kind of thing he'd get off on. Be just like Big Al.

Sammy didn't even consider denying the theft. It was true and Red knew it. "I swear, I don't have it anymore. But I can get it. I know who took it. My brother did. He came in here and took it."

"You're saying your fucking brother took it?"

"Yes. No, no, not exactly. He came to my house. I was keeping the money safe, and he took it."

"You're full of shit, Sammy. You always have been. I'm gonna break your fucking legs for you. I don't care who has the money now. I don't care what your problems are. Do I

172

look like a fucking shrink to you? Tell it to that cunt Ann Landers. You took it first. If he stole it from you, I don't give a shit. Steal it back. Steal it back and have it here on my fucking desk by tomorrow morning. Sell your mother's blood for nickels. Just get it back. Thirty-eight grand. That's what I figure you stole from me."

"My mother's dead."

"Yeah?" Red raised the baseball bat. "I guess you're shit out of luck." And swung the bat as Sammy tried desperately to move out of the way.

It brushed Sammy's back hard enough to sting like hell. Sammy screamed and rolled to the other side of Red's desk. The bat crashed down again, just missing him, splintering a corner of the desk into little slivers of wood that rained down onto Sammy's face. Red raised the bat again. Suddenly Sammy remembered his pistol. He felt like asking Red to hold on just a minute while he got it out. He clawed at his belt, couldn't find the gun at first, but finally got his hand on it. He pulled it out and pointed it at Red, just as Red was raising the Louisville Slugger like he was Reggie Jackson and it was the middle of October.

Red took one look at the pistol, saw that Sammy's hands were shaking, and started to laugh.

"Oh, shit, he's got a gun. Fucking little Sammy's got a gun. Help. What are you planning to do, Sammy, you gonna shoot me?" He tossed the baseball bat on the floor and walked nonchalantly over to his desk. When he got there he opened the drawer and pulled out a Colt .45. He turned to Sammy and said, "Now what, asshole? I got a gun too and mine's bigger than yours."

"Red, I don't want any trouble. Just drop the gun and let me leave. I'm sorry about the money. Just let me go."

"You ain't going anywhere. I changed my mind. I don't want my money back. Fuck that. It'd be worth paying thirty-eight grand just for the pleasure of shooting your miserable ass."

"Red, I'm serious." Sammy looked down at his own fingers. The hand that held the gun was trembling so much that he thought he might drop the pistol at any moment. He didn't know if he could even pull the trigger. It looked like someone else's hand, white and nervous, with the veins pulsing along his wrist like he had a blood-pressure cuff around his bicep. But he knew, if he let go of the gun, Red was going to kill him. He knew that for a fact.

The pistol in Red's hands was rock steady. He was enjoying himself, savoring the moment. He took two steps forward and extended the pistol so it almost touched Sammy's head. "World's gonna think your head blowing apart is a fucking backfire." He put the cold metal of the gun barrel on Sammy's scalp and added, "Oh, and Sam . . . you're fired."

Sammy wasn't sure what happened next. Something inside his head told him to move, and he did, sliding along the floor faster than anything he'd ever done before. He heard a tremendous explosion, as Red's pistol went off, and came up with his own gun pointed at Red's chest. He didn't even realize he'd pulled the trigger until he saw Red's body slam back against the wall and a big red stain erupt on Red's chest like a tropical flower in bloom.

Chapter

14

SAMMY LAY WHERE HE was on the floor for a long time, until his back started to cramp with the strain, and muscles in his hand and arm knotted up like thin snakes. His forehead was damp. He thought it might be his own blood, a thin trickle running down from his temple and onto his cheek. He touched his finger to it and realized it was sweat.

He pushed himself up from the floor, into a sitting position, and looked at Red. The other man was splayed out on the floor, his body slack, his neck twisted sideways, and one hand stretched out as if he was pointing at Sammy accusingly. There was a pool of blood on the floor underneath his chest and his tongue stuck halfway out of his mouth, as if his lips were dry and he'd been frozen in the act of licking them. His fingers were still clenched around the trigger of the gun.

Sammy kept expecting someone to come rushing into the room, the police, or one of Red's goons. No one did, and after a while he got up enough courage to stand. His back was killing him from where Red had hit him with the bat, but he managed to hobble over to Red's desk.

There was a safe behind the desk. Sammy knew the combination but now he couldn't remember it, couldn't get the numbers straight in his head long enough to spin the dial. Finally he decided, fuck it. He stood up and shot the dial of the safe. The piece of metal came flying back at him and nicked him in the arm. He dropped the pistol and grabbed his shoulder. It felt like someone was holding a hot poker against his biceps. But when he looked up the safe was open and he forgot the pain.

There was more money there than he'd ever seen in his life. Stacks of ten- and twenty-dollar bills, dozens of them, each wrapped with a rubber band. He forgot about being scared, forgot about killing Red or how much his back ached, thinking instead about all that newly orphaned money looking for a new home. Sweet Jesus, what he could do with it.

He turned finally, looking down at Red's corpse. He spat on it and said, "You thought I stole money from you, sat here and figured out that I took thirty-eight thousand dollars. You dumb fuck, you can't even add. It was over fifty grand. Over fifty grand I took from you. You can't count, you dumb bastard."

Laughing, feeling on top of the world all of a sudden, he scooped stacks of bills into his arms and thought about what it was like to be rich.

———

JOE DROVE to Red's pinball arcade and stopped his car across the street. He saw Sammy scurry out clutching a big garbage bag to his chest. He assumed Sammy must have gone and scored some dope off Red. It never entered his mind that anything else had happened, until he let himself into Red's office.

When he saw the dead man lying on the floor, he let out

176

a low whistle. He looked around the room. The safe in the corner was open and there wasn't a dime in it. What that meant was that Sammy, running out of there like he'd eaten chili peppers and was looking for a bathroom, carrying that garbage bag, Sammy'd had one hell of a night.

Joe was about to leave when he saw the wallet on the desk. He picked it up, went through the wallet, and smiled. He stood over Red, gazing down at the dead man, and said, "I'll tell you what, Red, dumb fuck Sammy could have drawn me a map, but I imagine this'll do just as well." He leaned down and poked Red in the ribs. "You want anything before I go? Glass of water? If not, I think I'll just head on down to this motel, see about getting your money back."

THERE WERE paper wrappers and plastic cups from fast-food places thrown in the back of Ben Costikyan's car. He had a cup of strong coffee in his hand and was smoking a cigar, chewing on the end and enjoying the mix, cheap cigar and black coffee. It felt good to be sitting there.

Across the street he could see the motel and a diner, the only place along the street with any activity. It was where Costikyan had gotten the coffee, chatting with a pretty little waitress and then heading back to his car, settling in to wait.

The sign by the motel was broken, red letters in the night that spelled out VA ANCY and flashed on and off. He could see a man behind the counter acting a little weird, like he was waiting for something to happen. Twice, since Costikyan had gotten his coffee, the guy had walked out to the street and looked back and forth. A car pulled up slowly and parked in the motel lot. Costikyan moved forward in his seat to get a better view. He saw one person get out of the car, but he couldn't tell who it was until the man stepped into the pool of light near the motel office. It was Jjaks Clayton.

The lieutenant put his coffee cup on the dashboard and

said softly, "Hot damn, look at what we got here. Mr. Jjaks Clayton. What'd we do, Jjaks, we forget to return our room key?"

He felt like a fox outside of a chicken coop.

———

JJAKS WAS at the office of the motel manager. The manager looked like he was going to have a coronary. Nervous but greedy at the same time.

The manager said, "You got here fast."

"You said by morning."

The man strutted a little. "Yeah, I guess I did."

His wife was there, a woman in her fifties wearing a polyester pantsuit and too much makeup. She asked, "Would you like a cup of tea?"

"No."

The manager asked, "A sandwich?"

"No."

"Your brother parking the car?"

He's not here yet."

"Whatd'ya mean? Where is he?"

"Relax. He's getting the money. He'll be along."

"He'll be along?"

"I told you I'd get the money. I'm here to tell you that it's going to happen, okay? My brother is out getting the money. Everything is going to work out fine." He walked over and peered out the window. "What's your name?"

"Frank."

"Frank, you got to go with me on this. We can work it out, but you got to get a grip."

"Your brother's getting the money?"

Jjaks tried smiling. It didn't quite come off, but he said, "That's what I told you."

"How?"

"Just relax, okay? He'll be here shortly."

"You trust him?"

Jjaks managed to look surprised. "Do I trust him? He's my brother."

"Right, right."

"Everything's cool."

"Right, I'll relax."

There was a magazine rack by the front desk. Jjaks wandered over to see if there was anything he could look at to kill time. He didn't know when Sammy would get there, but he wanted the manager to think everything was going fine, wanted the man to see that he wasn't concerned.

There were travel brochures, maps, and a couple of old magazines. Jjaks picked up a six-month-old copy of *Sports Illustrated* and sat down on a cracked leather couch by the door. As he did so a shiny object caught his eyes and he glanced past the manager's feet to the hallway leading to the living quarters of the office. There was something on the floor. Something gold. Jjaks looked away, it wasn't important, but a second later he found himself glancing back. It was familiar, whatever it was, something he'd seen before.

He stood up. The manager was nervously pacing back and forth. He stopped moving when Jjaks took a step in the direction of the hallway.

"What are you doing?"

"Frank, you go back to wearing out the carpet. Don't worry, if I'm thinking of taking a stroll." He was halfway across the room; the shiny object was bigger. He stepped past Frank.

"Stop . . . you can't . . ."

Jjaks turned. There must've been something in his face because Frank shut his mouth and stood there quietly.

Jjaks realized what it was before he actually touched it. It didn't make sense. It was a locket, a little gold heart on a thin gold chain that he'd last seen on Freddie's neck.

He picked it up, holding it in front of his eyes. What the fuck was going on here?

Behind him, the manager swore in a scared voice and

179

then said, "Look, it wasn't my idea. I just try to run a business."

"Shut up."

"It wasn't my idea."

"Shut the fuck up." Jjaks rushed over to the man and grabbed him in a headlock, pulling tightly on his neck until he could see the veins swell in the man's forehead. He shouted, "What the fuck is going on here? Where'd you get this? Answer me, goddammit, you have to answer me."

Behind him he could hear the manager's wife start to scream. He whirled the manager in a circle and crashed him into the door of the motel office. The woman's screams were even louder as Jjaks and the manager crashed out onto the road.

Jjaks got to his feet. The manager was yelling, "Help, help." Jjaks grabbed him and drew back his fist. All he wanted to do was bury it in the man's face, feel flesh against his knuckles. The manager made sucking noises in his throat and seemed unable to talk.

Jjaks screamed, "You took her body, you sick son of a bitch. Where is she? You followed me and dug her up. That's what this is." He held his hand up in the air. "This was Freddie's locket. You brought her back here, whatever, and you must've dropped this."

"No . . . no . . . that's not what happened."

Jjaks could hear someone calling his name. He didn't pay any attention at first. He wanted to kill the man. But then the voice called again and Jjaks' blood seemed to freeze in his veins.

It stopped him dead, made hairs on the back of his neck stand straight up and a cold wave of chills run down his spine, popping goose bumps on his skin. He pivoted slowly, afraid of what he might see.

Freddie was standing across the street in front of the diner.

The manager said, "She put us up to it. We saw what we

saw, but we weren't going to get involved. All we knew, like I told you, was one of you carried her in and the other carried her out. All bloody. It's not my business. But she's not dead and she said we could make a little money. . . ."

Jjaks said, "Shut up."

". . . the thing is we're really tired of the motel business. There's no future in it, you know. We had our eyes on this really nice RV, used, and—" He stopped talking as Freddie reached Jjaks.

A part of Jjaks was so freaked out he wanted to run, and keep running, until he was as far away from her as possible. But another part of him was overjoyed to see her. Wanted to run into her arms.

She spoke. "It's all right, baby. Don't worry, I know what happened. I know it was Sammy who killed me."

"Oh, God." He felt his knees weakening. Felt a swirl of black fog come rushing toward him. Freddie's image began to blur as his legs buckled and he hit the floor.

———

HE CAME to with Freddie holding his head in her arms and smacking him in the face. At first he thought he'd been dreaming, Freddie getting shot and him burying her by the side of the road. Then he thought the other had been a dream. That, in fact, she was still dead and the experience in the motel had been fantasy. He opened his eyes, though, and there she was.

"It's okay, Jjaks. I'm here."

He put his arms around her. Just the sight of her, the realization that she was alive, was enough to lift his spirits. He said, "Ahhh, Freddie . . ."

They stayed like that for a long time, without speaking. Holding each other until Freddie pulled back. Her face was twisted in pain.

Jjaks asked, "Are you sure you're all right?"

"I'll be okay. It hurts a little, is all. Where Sammy shot me. I'll be fine, though."

"You sure?"

"Yeah. The bullet went all the way through me." There was a quarter-sized patch of blood on her shirt. She pulled the shirt up and showed him a bandage and then pulled the edges of the bandage away. He could see the bullet hole. She said, "It's okay. I'm fine. Sam's a lousy shot. It knocked me out, that's why you thought I was dead. The doctor said I was lucky, but I told him there was no such thing as luck."

"I don't understand. What happened? I thought you were dead. I was sure of it."

"Someone found me by the side of the road."

Jjaks put his face in his hands. "I thought I buried you. Jesus."

"A trucker found me. He saved my life."

He saw something glistening on the side of her head and moved into the light. "Shit, you're bleeding. We have to get you to a hospital."

"No, no hospital. It's not that bad."

"I never thought I'd see you again. It's real. Right? It must be. I mean, I've never felt like . . . whatever that word is. Happy? I never dreamed I'd see you again."

"I know. I never thought I'd see you either. The last thing I remember is being in the car with Sammy. He had a gun and forced me to drive. Then . . . he shot me. I don't know anything after that."

"I'm gonna get him."

"Don't worry about that now. Just tell me what happened."

"I don't know exactly. My ear was killing me. I drank too much and blacked out. Next thing I knew, you were in the bathroom and I thought you were dead. The cops were everywhere."

"What'd you do?"

He grinned. "I put you in bed. Told them you were asleep."

"Not bad."

"I thought I'd killed you."

She touched his face, running her fingers along his cheek. "Why would you want to kill me?"

"I wouldn't."

"Damn right. What'd I ever do to you?"

"Nothing."

"So why would you think you had killed me? It was Sammy."

"But I thought . . ."

"I know . . . and it's all right."

"Just thinking about you . . . under dirt and leaves. Shit."

"You broke my heart, Jjaks."

"I was scared. I was stupid. Please forgive me."

"Baby, I've already forgiven you. Believe me, if I hadn't, you'd be dead."

She leaned slowly into his arms and put her lips against his. He thought she was the most beautiful woman he'd ever seen and all he wanted to do was hold on to her.

~~~

SAMMY DROVE to the motel. It was as if he was glued to the seat. He saw Jjaks' car. There was no sign of anyone else. All he could do was sit and stare at the car.

He had a picture of what would happen. He'd go in there and hand the money over. Give all this cash to some schmuck who thought blackmail was a way to make a living. Why? To get Jjaks off the hook. Maybe get himself off the hook too. But, the thing was, if he had all this cash, he didn't need to get off the hook. He could go anywhere in the world, spend the money, and not worry about anybody finding him.

He saw movement. Jjaks, or the manager, he couldn't tell who, stepped in front of the window.

It had started to drizzle, a thin mist that came down slowly and looked like heavy fog as it passed by the light from the street lamp. It covered the windshield every few minutes. He had to turn the wipers on, wait for them to clear the glass before he went back to watching the motel.

He was thinking about getting out, walking around. It would be stupid to sit there until someone spotted him. What he needed was a little time to think. Maybe he'd get a bite to eat and a cup of coffee. He could relax, consider his options.

Why not? Sammy drove across the street to the twenty-four-hour diner.

COSTIKYAN SAW Sammy pull in and said to himself, Here we go. He watched Sammy sit there, staring at the motel. He expected Sammy to go inside. When he did, Costikyan would take the next step.

But it never happened. Sammy sat for five minutes and then drove across the street and went into the diner.

It took the lieutenant by surprise. Jjaks was at the motel and Sammy had driven there. Why didn't he go in? It was the logical thing to do. Instead, Sammy went across the street. To do what? Watch and wait?

The lieutenant lit another cigar. Sammy wanted to wait? No big fucking deal. It was something Costikyan was fairly good at himself. He'd had a lot of practice over the years. He took a drag of his cigar, enjoying himself. Feeling the first real stirrings of anticipation in his gut.

THE WAITRESS called out, "You ever find your horse?" She'd been at the far end of the counter, serving coffee to an old geezer in a filthy undershirt and blue pants with a yellow stripe down the side. He looked like some kind of half-dressed, sorry-assed doorman.

When she was finished, she strolled over to Sammy, put a cup of coffee in front of him, and asked, "Well?"

What the hell was she talking about? Then he remembered. "The horse. The one that danced?"

"Yeah, why, you got more than one?"

"No, just the one. He got away."

"She."

"What?"

"You said its name was Clementine."

"I did?"

"Of course. Wait, it was written on the side of that thing—what do you call it—the cart that the horse travels in."

"A horse cart?"

"I guess." She looked past him, staring outside like the horse trailer was still there. "I remember. It said Clementine. How come, if it was your horse, how come you didn't even know its name?"

Sammy put the coffee cup down and leaned forward.

The waitress looked around like she didn't want anyone overhearing either, and then she too leaned over the counter.

Sammy whispered, "Can I tell you something?"

"What?"

"What if I told you I knew someone who had enough money, if he wanted to buy a horse, he could just go out and buy one. Shit, he could buy a dozen."

She stepped back, considering it. Sammy watched her. He found himself comparing her with Freddie. Where Freddie had seemed wild, this girl seemed sensible.

Shit, he liked it here, sitting in this diner. It didn't matter if it was a dive, that a man in old doorman's trousers and a dirty undershirt shared the same counter as he did. The girl in front of him was nice. She could work in a place like this

185

and still smile, be pleasant. Plus, she wasn't bad looking. Maybe not smoldering gorgeous, like Freddie. But fuck Freddie, she was dead for one thing, and even when she was alive she hadn't been such a prize. Jjaks could have her, except that would have made Jjaks happy and Sammy didn't want that.

All things considered it wasn't a bad deal that Freddie was dead.

This girl liked horses so much, maybe Sammy would buy her one someday. She was chewing gum. Sammy watched her jaw move and then said, "Lemme ask you a question."

"Sure." Working her mouth to an inner beat. It didn't take anything away from her. In fact, Sammy thought it made her look cuter.

She chomped for a moment and then said, "You want me to throw that out?" Pointing at the garbage bag. Sammy grabbed the bag and hugged it to him.

"No, that's all right. I got . . . I got stuff in there."

"Geez, you okay?"

"Yeah."

"You sure?"

"I'm fine. Just let me ask you something."

"Shoot."

"Okay . . . if you . . . say you did something bad. . . ."

"Like what?"

"I don't know . . . say . . . imagine you killed someone." Sammy shook his head violently. "No, say you killed two people. Okay? Murdered them. But in the process of doing that, killing them, you had gotten almost a hundred grand, that's ninety-eight thousand dollars, which nobody was gonna miss, and there was a stranger blackmailing you." He took a deep breath. "Would you give him back a chunk of that money? Even if you worked pretty hard to get it?"

He wasn't sure if what he said made any sense. It didn't look like it from what he could tell. She was staring at him, leaning her elbows on the counter with her chin resting on one hand. Giving him a long look.

Eventually she asked, "Is this a joke?"

He shook his head.

"You're weird, you know that? I think you're nice. I only met you yesterday. But you're a weird one."

"Did you understand what I said? About the money?"

"Sure. That part was easy. Some guy wants to take your money. And you killed somebody to get it in the first place. Did I get it right?"

"More or less."

"Is this for real?"

"Look, what difference does it make? Could be, all it is, is one of those hypochondriac things. . . ."

"Hypothetical."

"What?"

"You mean, where you make something up as an example? So you can say, 'What if this happened?' "

"Yeah, right."

"That means it's hypothetical."

"That's what I said."

"Oh." She smiled.

Sammy looked at her to see if she was making fun of him, but she seemed totally serious. "So what would you do?"

"What would I do? Hmm." She took a strand of her hair in her hand, twirling it around a finger absentmindedly. "I think . . ."

"Yes?"

"I think I'd tell the person that he wasn't going to get one red cent."

"You mean, the guy who's blackmailing me?"

"Yeah. What right does he have to the money?"

Sammy nodded. "Yeah. He doesn't have any fucking right at all." He saw the look on her face and said, "Excuse my language."

"It's all right. I can tell you're mad. I don't blame you."

"You don't?"

"I'd be mad too."

"You would?"

She leaned all the way over the counter until she was almost touching his ear with her lips and grinned. He could smell spearmint and a touch of perfume. She whispered, "You wanna know what?" She giggled.

"What?"

"I definitely wouldn't give the bastard one red cent."

―――

JJAKS WAS learning how to play chess. He was sitting across a small table from Frank, the motel manager. There was a cheap plastic chess set between them and Frank had been trying to explain the game for the last twenty minutes. The man was nervous, Jjaks could see it. He kept looking away from the board to glance at Freddie or out the window at the street.

Jjaks had to say, "Frank, you want to pay attention here?" He had his hand on the knight. "Tell me again."

"Like an L. One up and two over or two up and one over."

Jjaks put the piece back on the board and tried moving it in several different directions. "You sure? It doesn't make a lot of sense. Why not just go straight ahead, run over another piece. It's a horse, right? Kick some ass with it, that's what I'd do."

The manager sighed. "I didn't invent the game. I just play it."

Freddie was in a chair in the corner, watching them play, with a frustrated look on her face. She glanced at the clock. "Is that all you two are gonna do? Play a fucking game?"

Jjaks smiled at her. "Hon, it's all we can do. We have to wait until Sammy gets here."

"You're crazy to be depending on him. He tried to kill me."

188

Jjaks went back to his chess piece, saying softly, "We'll get to that when the time comes."

"I can't take it. Where the hell is he?"

The manager said, "She's right. He should have been here by now. I don't want any trouble. I just want to get this over with."

Jjaks grinned. "You don't want any trouble? You agreed to blackmail me and now you're worried about trouble. Whoo-ee."

The manager pointed at Freddie. "I only did it because she told me to."

"What'd she do, twist your arm?"

Freddie laughed. "I asked him and he jumped at the chance. I didn't need to twist anything."

Jjaks smiled at the manager. "Well, there you are." He picked up a rook. "This guy, he goes on his own color. Diagonal?"

"What? No, he can move back and forth. Straight across or straight forward. The bishop goes diagonal. Stays on his own color."

Jjaks picked up the queen. "The bishop?"

Freddie said, "Shit, I've got to take a walk. I can't stand this."

Jjaks said, "Back in prison, we played checkers. You didn't have to remember so much."

"If I tell you something," the manager asked, "you won't be offended? I gotta tell you."

"So?"

"I'm not up for playing this game with you."

"Why not?"

"For one thing, you're not even trying."

Freddie said loudly, "Jjaks, I'm serious. I don't know how much longer I can take this."

"It'll be all right. Just give it some time."

"Where the fuck is Sammy? I can't hang around here in paradise for the rest of my life."

Frank said, "Me too. She's right. It's been a while."

Jjaks glared at him. "I got an idea, whyn't you give some thought to keeping your mouth shut. Turn down the volume a bit." He turned to Freddie. "We could leave now. Just leave and be all right, just the two of us."

"I can't, Jjaks. You know me, I need to do things, and see things. For real, not for shit. That money's my ticket out of here. You wouldn't want me to leave without it, not after everything that's happened? Would you?"

"Listen to your girlfriend," the manager said.

"You really are starting to get on my nerves," Jjaks glanced at Freddie. She was moving toward the door. He got up out of his chair and hurried over to her. "Where are you going?"

"I am hungry," Freddie said. "I got a fucking hole in my stomach. And I'm tired of waiting. You want something to eat? I'll bring you back something to eat."

Jjaks watched her go. When she was safely inside the diner, he sat back down. The manager had a sour look on his face, half frustration and half fear. Jjaks reached over and punched him on the shoulder lightly. He picked up a pawn and asked, "This one, what is it again, is this the king?"

Chapter 15

SAMMY HAD TO LISTEN to the manager say, "Twin City Motel. Twenty-one ninety-five gets you a double bed and free cable TV. How can I help you?"

"You can put my fucking brother on the phone, asshole."

Sammy was in the phone booth at the far end of the counter. He glanced up and saw the waitress watching him. He waved and then heard Jjaks' voice on the line.

Jjaks said, "Yeah?"

"It's me."

"You get the money?"

"I got it all right."

"So what are you waiting for? Come on over and we can get this shit over with. And, oh yeah, bring the key."

"What key?"

"The motel key. On top of everything, this guy wants his key back. He says either I give him the room key back or he's gonna charge me thirty bucks. It's in the fish dish by your TV. I saw it there."

"I'm not at the house, Jjaks."

"What? Where are you?"

There was a long pause and then Sammy spoke as if Jjaks had never asked the question. "You should have seen me, Jjaks. I was good. Hell, I was fucking great. Guy treated me like shit ever since the day I started to work for him. Well, he's not treating me like shit no more."

"Sammy, that's good. Thing is, we're sitting here—"

"Motherfucker won't be treating anyone like shit."

"Good. Listen, we'll see you soon. You on your way?"

"Jjaks, I got to tell you, I can see it. You're sitting in that dump of a motel. Am I right?"

"You know where I am."

"I can picture it." He leaned out of the booth and looked across the street. It gave him an incredible feeling of power, knowing Jjaks was right over there and didn't have any idea that Sammy could see him. "You like that motel?"

"What?"

"I mean, is it your kind of place?"

"Sammy, what the fuck are you doing? Just bring the money and come on over."

"I don't think so."

"Sammy, this guy will dime you out just like me. He saw both of us."

"Nobody saw me, Jjaks." He turned to look for the waitress, wanting to see her face when he finally told Jjaks off.

She was waiting on someone over by the take-out counter. He couldn't see who it was. He spoke into the phone again. "Jjaks, you remember when I held your hand on the stove?"

"You think I'd forget that?"

"Well . . ." He looked for the waitress. His new girlfriend. He was planning to take her home with him, or wherever he decided to go with all that money. She was ringing up the register, turning slowly to hand someone change. A woman, with her back to Sammy.

192

Sammy talked into the phone, trying to check out the woman at the same time. "I'm gonna burn you again, Jjaks. . . ." His eyes traveled up the woman's legs, admiring them. He saw the waitress smile at the other woman. Damn, now the woman had moved and a jukebox was blocking Sammy's view.

He said, "That's right, Jjaks, I'm gonna burn you all over again. . . ." and then started to repeat the word *burn*, over and over in his head, because the customer had turned and taken a step toward the door.

Sammy felt the blood in his veins turn to ice water. He felt like a store mannequin, unable to move. He stopped talking altogether because he was seeing Freddie, alive and well, getting her change, picking up a bag of doughnuts and then walking jauntily out of the diner. He watched her cross the street, with his mouth hanging open in astonishment.

He saw her go over to the motel office, knock, and go in. Then he screamed into the phone, "*Jjjjaaaakkkkssss . . .*" Sammy slammed the phone down and took off with the garbage bag full of money, startling the old man in the striped trousers and causing the waitress to drop a cup of coffee.

He banged against the door and hurried across the street.

Jjaks was staring at the phone when Freddie knocked. The manager let her in. She walked right over to Jjaks and asked, "What's the matter?"

"I don't know. That was Sammy. . . ."

"He have the money?"

"He said he did. I was talking to him. . . ."

"Well . . . ?"

"Well, what?"

"Is he bringing the money?" There was intensity to her voice that he hadn't noticed before. An anxious look on her face that had nothing to do with sitting in this shitty little motel office and everything in the world with never having to sit in one again.

193

He said slowly, "I think he hung up."

"*What?*"

"I was talking to him one second and then it was like he wasn't there. He screamed and then nothing."

"You think maybe Red got him? Or one of his guys?"

Jjaks stopped to think it over. "No, I don't think so. I mean, he said he had the money. That it was fine. He said . . . 'The guy ain't ever gonna treat anyone like a piece of shit again.' Who's he mean—Red?"

"I guess. That's who he went to get the money from."

"It isn't like Red's just going to give it to him. But I can't picture Sammy taking it."

Freddie pointed at her stomach. "No? You have any trouble picturing Sammy doing this to me? That son of a bitch didn't have any qualms about shooting me."

"Yeah, but, I don't know, Sammy seems . . . so wimpy."

"So what if he is? That's what people do, they get scared. The next thing you know they're pulling out a gun. How much courage does it take to pull a trigger?"

"I don't know."

"*You* don't. But Sammy does."

She took a sip of her coffee and then spit it out. "Dammit. I told that waitress I wanted sugar. I got to go all the way back there and get some." She stepped to the door and opened it. The next thing Jjaks heard was the sound of Freddie's quick scream and he looked up to see Sammy in the doorway.

Sammy looked like a man possessed by the devil. His hair was sticking up at crazy angles, as if he'd showered and then stuck his head into the blades of a running fan. He held a gun in one hand and a plastic garbage bag in the other. He pointed the gun at Jjaks and clutched the bag to his chest like he was thinking of fucking it.

He stared from Freddie to Jjaks and then yelled at the top of his lungs. "*What the hell did you do to me?*"

Freddie took one look at him, the expression on his face

and the way he was waving the gun around, and screamed. Jjaks stared at her in amazement. He'd never heard anyone scream that loudly before. The sound seemed to go on and on, and when she finally stopped, it was as if someone had flipped a switch, turned a powerful stereo off. The silence was deafening.

Sammy said, "What the fuck are you screaming at? You're acting like *you* just saw a ghost, but it's me that's seen the ghost." He walked toward Freddie, carrying the gun and the garbage bag. When he got to her he reached out slowly and touched her sleeve.

"You get your fucking hands off me." She slapped at his hand.

Jjaks said, "You got it, Sammy, she's real. She's alive."

"She can't be. She can't. I killed her, I know I did."

Jjaks took a step toward his brother. He wanted to take that pistol away from Sammy and stick it down his throat. "Whatcha got in the bag, Sammy?" His brother pulled the bag closer. "Is that the money, Sam? You figuring, what, you came here to do the deal or are you thinking of keeping it for yourself?"

Sammy had been glancing back and forth from Jjaks to Freddie. Now he looked at Jjaks and said, "I don't remember you goin' out and getting it. When I had to walk into Red's office, I don't recall you being behind me."

Jjaks said, "Jesus."

"What?" Freddie was done screaming and was listening to what they were saying.

Jjaks said, "He's gonna keep it."

"The money?"

Sammy laughed at her. "Bright girl."

Freddie started to talk louder. Jjaks was afraid she was going to start screaming again any minute. His one good ear couldn't take it. She said, "Whatta you mean he's going to take it? That's my fucking money."

Behind them, the motel manager snapped his fingers.

"Leave us not forget, we're in my office. I put some time in on this, some of that money belongs to me."

Freddie said, "Shut the fuck up. You're gonna be lucky to get out of this alive." She turned to Jjaks. "Baby, you can't let him."

"He's got a gun."

"Fucking right I do," Sammy said.

"Jjaks . . . do something." It sounded like if he didn't do something, she would, and he thought her idea of doing something could get them both killed. He looked at his brother.

"What do you plan to do, Sammy? You going to kill us all? You don't have to. You got enough in the bag for all of us."

Sam looked around the room with his eyes starting to go a little wild. Jjaks knew what he was doing. He was psyching himself up, getting primed to aim that pistol and start pulling the trigger. He'd seen cons do it in the federal penitentiary, jazz themselves up and then go stick a shank in somebody's back.

Watching Sammy, Jjaks realized that he'd never felt less like the man's brother than now. Even when Sammy was holding his hand on the hot burner, all those years ago, even then, Jjaks felt something, some sort of bond. Not now. He looked across the six feet of motel office separating them and all he saw was a common thief. A murderer.

Sammy pointed at the ceiling with his gun and said, "Oh boy . . . you know . . . how does something like this happen to me? I went and got the police. Jesus, they must think I'm an asshole. It never occurred to me. I thought about it a lot, what happened. I assumed someone moved the body." He looked at Jjaks. "I thought you had. But I couldn't figure out how or when. It just never occurred to me that the reason your body was missing was 'cause you weren't dead."

Freddie said, "Yeah, well, I'm not."

"Not for long maybe."

196

Jjaks said, "I'll tell you what, you go along. Take the fucking money and leave. I don't give a shit."

Freddie yelled, "Don't listen to him." She said to Jjaks, "He's not going anywhere with that money." She stepped up to Sammy and put her hand on his arm. "Sam, you got a lot of money in there, right?"

"Yeah. I do." He was grinning now.

"Don't you think, if you've got a lot of money, a *lot*, isn't there enough that we can share it?"

He burst out laughing. "You are a trip. You know that, Freddie? You walk out on my wedding day. Shack up with my own brother, and now you're asking do I want to share something with you. Goddamn, girl." He pushed her away and waved the gun at Jjaks. "How 'bout you, you wanna share? You shared my wife, you might think you're entitled to my money."

Jjaks shrugged. "I already told you, the door's right there. You want to walk out, that's okay."

"Yeah? You're gonna let me walk out. Fuck you, you think I need your permission?" He raised the gun. Suddenly Jjaks didn't have any doubt that he was capable of using it. The end of the pistol looked enormous, a black hole that seemed to fill the room, suck the oxygen right out of the air.

The door behind them burst open and Joe came in low, with his gun drawn. He had a look of satisfaction on his face and a pistol in his hand. Sammy took one look at him and squeezed off a quick shot that caught the man in the middle of the forehead and dropped him like a stone. The manager's wife started to scream. "I don't wanna die, please. Just leave us alone. I don't want any money."

Jjaks heard the motel manager hiccup in fear and Freddie burst out in tears. She moaned, "You're going to do it again, aren't you? You're just going to kill me again. Aren't you, Sam?" She was weeping now.

Sammy stayed in the same position, gun held out and his

eyes locked on Jjaks'. He smiled slowly. "Did I tell you I have a girlfriend?" he asked.

When Jjaks didn't answer, he nodded. "That's right. I got a girlfriend." He jerked his head in the direction of the twenty-four-hour diner. "She works over there. Sweetest little thing you'll ever see."

Jjaks said, "Yeah?" Measuring the distance in his head. Getting it straight, how he was going to try it. He could feint one way, see if Sammy pulled the trigger and missed, maybe it would throw him off balance, and then Jjaks could come in and tackle him. He was talking just to keep it from happening until he was ready.

He said, "So, you got a girl? You hear that, Freddie?" She was still weeping, paying no attention. "Sammy's got himself a woman."

Sammy nodded. "She's no slut either. Like some people I could talk about. This girl's got quality. Doesn't like people that swear. She and I are going to get horses. Lots of horses."

"Horses?" Jjaks was going to blow it because the idea of Sammy owning a horse was ludicrous.

"What are you smiling about? You think it's funny?" Sammy swung the gun until it was pointed at the motel manager's head. "What about you? You think horses are funny too?"

The manager was white with fear. He shook his head as fast as possible and said, "Horses are nice. They're dandy. I'd get one of my own if I could."

"Shut the fuck up," Sammy told him. "Nobody's asking you." He looked at Jjaks. "I should have done this a long time ago."

Jjaks could feel Freddie watching. She'd stopped crying, whether out of fear or curiosity he couldn't tell. But he had a vague impression of her, sitting calmly on the floor now, watching both of them as Sammy raised his gun and pressed his finger against the trigger until everyone could see it turn white. There was a loud bang and Jjaks felt something hit him in the stomach hard. When he looked down, there was a hole in his belly and a crimson stain spreading on his shirt.

BEN COSTIKYAN wanted to be able to see in there, get inside that motel, and find out who was doing what to . . . to anybody.

Right about now he thought he'd go on over and see if it was done. Go see what the boys were doing in that motel office.

He moved his bulk out of the car, made sure his gun was in his holster, and started to walk across the street. Suddenly he heard the unmistakable sound of a gunshot.

He started to run.

Jjaks couldn't believe it. He could reach down and stick his finger in his belly, which might not be too bad of an idea because it was bleeding. There was a steady ooze, like water out of a spring, about three inches to the right of his belly button. It shocked the hell out of him. The manager was yelling in terror, a high keening sound that seemed somehow inappropriate for a man his size. Jjaks thought about telling him to knock it off, but he was too busy staring at his stomach.

He was on the floor, sitting there with a stupid look on his face because when Sammy had pulled the trigger, the force of the bullet had knocked Jjaks back. Then he'd sat the rest of the way down in surprise. There wasn't a lot of pain, just a burning sensation that worked its way down Jjaks' stomach and along the nerves of his right leg. He experimented with his limbs, breathing a little easier because he could move them all.

He glanced from the wound to his brother. Sammy had a shit-eating but fairly surprised look on his face. It seemed as if he was as shocked as anyone that the gun had gone off,

199

but now that it had, he was beginning to consider shooting again. Even as Jjaks watched, a look of profound triumph settled on Sammy's face and he looked from the gun to his brother.

"There, how's it feel now? You think you're gonna jump up, take my wife again?"

Jjaks felt almost too tired to answer. Sammy's voice seemed to get loud and soft for no apparent reason. He realized that the edges of the room, the outer limits of his vision, were becoming blurred. He thought if somebody didn't do something, call for help soon, he might be in a spot of trouble.

Freddie had begun to crawl slowly across the floor to the back end of the motel office where the hallway led to the exit. Sammy watched her progress. When she was three quarters of the way there, he raised the gun again. Jjaks saw him do it and made a desperate lunge. He banged into Sammy's legs, throwing his brother off balance just as he pulled the trigger. The bullet smashed through the chessboard on the coffee table, splintering the wall inches from Freddie's face. She screamed and stopped moving. Jjaks used all of his strength to drag Sammy to the ground. He locked his hands on the gun in Sammy's hand and tried to pry it out of Sammy's fingers. Sammy was trying to turn the gun toward Jjaks and Jjaks knew that he had only one chance to get it away from him before his strength started to fade. He brought his knee up and tried to slam it between Sammy's legs, but his brother twisted out of his way. Jjaks pushed against the table behind him for leverage, and as he did Sammy gave a violent twist of his body and tried to spin away. There was an earsplitting bang, the smell of gunpowder, and a stricken look came over Sammy's face.

He let go of Jjaks and fell back to the floor.

Sammy mumbled, "Jesus, I'm shot." And the door blew open behind him and Ben Costikyan stepped into the office.

200

The manager's wife screamed, "No more. Please, no more."

Costikyan said, "It's all right. I'm a police officer."

Jjaks reached slowly out and picked the pistol up from the floor near his brother's body.

Costikyan said, "Don't anybody move a goddamn muscle."

There was silence, except for the heavy breathing of the lieutenant and soft whimpering from the hotel manager. Freddie was across from Jjaks. It crossed his mind to try to crawl over to her, but she wasn't looking at him. She was staring at Sammy's body. There was a thin curl of smoke rising from where the bullet had entered his body.

Costikyan squatted down on his haunches and said to Freddie, "Come here, honey." He said to Jjaks, "Put the gun down, Jjaks."

Freddie had a strange look on her face, as if she knew what she was supposed to do but was torn. Costikyan said, "Come on, Freddie, come here."

"I don't think I can."

"Come here."

Jjaks asked, "Freddie?"

Costikyan had stood up. He walked over to the garbage bag and looked inside. Jjaks could see the corners of bills sticking out. Costikyan grinned. "Hell, there's more here than I hoped."

When he stood back up he turned to the motel manager and barked, "You?"

"Yes . . . ?"

"This is now officially a police crime scene." He dug in his jacket and produced a badge. "What I'm going to ask you . . . no, wait . . . I'm gonna tell you, you and your wife, is to go outside and wait. I need to . . . process the scene. So get your sorry ass out in the street and don't talk to nobody about nothin'. You understand?"

The motel manager nodded but didn't go anywhere until

the lieutenant screamed, "Now, you motherfucker. I'm talking, *right now.*"

When the couple had left, Costikyan pulled a cigar out of his pocket. He smiled at Jjaks and said, "You mind?" and went ahead and lit the cigar without waiting for Jjaks to speak. After he had it going, he walked over, reached down, and put his hand under Freddie's chin. She was as still as a statue, staring into the lieutenant's face like a lost child. When she was looking directly into his eyes, Costikyan spoke again. "Freddie, you got one corpse already."

Freddie said, "I don't know if I can go through with this."

Costikyan said, "Go through with it? It's done."

He leaned down. "It's gonna be nice. You'll see." He pointed at Jjaks. "You got your good friend over there, he's wondering, right now, what's gonna happen to him. Maybe I'm gonna shoot him. It's probably what he expects, 'cause he's a realist. He can tell when it doesn't matter anymore, when things get so out of hand that it just doesn't make sense to raise a fuss." He smiled at Jjaks. "Am I right, boy?"

Jjaks spat in his direction and said, "Kiss my ass."

"No, I don't think so. I done all the ass kissing I'm ever gonna do." He put his hand on Freddie's hair and stroked it.

Freddie looked at Jjaks finally. She said in a flat voice, "What'd you expect, Jjaks, we'd go riding off into the sunset?"

Jjaks said, "Don't do it, Freddie."

Costikyan said, "See, Freddie, he doesn't know what's best for you. He's thinking of himself, is all. You and I, we got to think about what's best for you. We're gonna wrap this thing up in a nice, neat package. Let the Clayton brothers take credit for the whole shebang. 'Cause it's done. I'm not gonna fuck with you. The truth is, you don't have a choice. You want lover boy over there to live, then it's a done deal. Otherwise, I may get mad, ace you both." He pointed at Jjaks. "That boy there, him and his brother, hell, honey, they shot and buried you."

She looked at Jjaks. He looked like he wanted to tell her not to do it, to forget about whatever had happened in the past. Not to think about who shot who and did he make an attempt to bury her just because he'd thought she was dead.

She said, "Jjaks, it wasn't going to work." She thought she could hear something in her own voice, a pleading note. She whispered, "I don't know what I thought, what you thought. But it doesn't happen like that. It just doesn't."

Jjaks raised himself up on one elbow. He felt weak and wondered whether the bullet from Sammy's gun had done some irreparable damage, torn away his guts, and it was only a matter of time before it killed him. It didn't matter that much. He said, "Freddie, don't do it. He's an animal. He'll make your life a living hell."

She snapped, "Yeah, and what were you going to do?" She looked around the room. "This is as far as I would've gotten with you. Shitty little motel rooms, creepy places."

He wondered, was this how it would work? She'd talk herself into accepting whatever Costikyan had in mind for her?

Costikyan said, "Baby, you tell him." He leaned forward and draped a hand on her shoulder. It looked huge, like a grizzly bear's paw, against the thinness of Freddie's arm. Costikyan was grinning at Jjaks. "I'll tell you what, son, you might get lucky here, live long enough to go to trial."

Jjaks shook his head, but he felt powerless. "I'm never going back to jail."

The lieutenant stood up. "Fuck you ain't, boy." He took one more look around the room and then repeated himself. "The fuck you ain't. Unless you want to die right here." He raised the pistol until it was pointed at Jjaks' head.

Freddie said, "Don't do it, please." Costikyan glanced in her direction and she tried to smile. "Please, don't do it . . . Ben. Leave him alone."

"It's all right. I'm not going to hurt him anymore. He's in enough trouble as it is."

203

There was a tiny movement from Sammy, a slight exhalation of breath and a twitch. Costikyan shook his head. "Goddammit." He left Freddie, walked over to Sammy's body, and put his hand carefully over Sammy's nose and mouth. Sammy twitched slightly, a dying convulsion. Costikyan leaned his knee on Sammy's chest and stayed that way until long after any movement stopped.

He looked at Jjaks. "Fucking A. Jjaks, if you're gonna kill someone . . . then you oughta kill them."

Jjaks could feel Freddie's eyes on him. He didn't want to look at her, but eventually he did. He saw a single tear form and trickle down her cheek.

She said, "Jjaks . . . you have to understand. That's all . . . you just have to understand."

Chapter 16

THEY WHEELED HIM THROUGH the doors to the emergency room, two paramedics and a cop. The cop kept asking him what happened, did he know who had shot him, Jjaks kept saying, yeah, he knew who it was, all right. It was a cop. Jjaks' head wasn't too clear, he was having trouble following the conversation, and he felt colder than hell. He said to one of the paramedics, "I think it was a cop. I don't know, it could have been my brother." Above him the fluorescent lights were flashing by, like windows in a train on a moonless night, fast enough that he couldn't quite focus on any one of them.

The cop had a notebook in his hand; he was leaning down to hear Jjaks, trotting to keep up. Jjaks told him, "My brother's name is Sammy. You find the hottest-looking woman you've ever seen, ask her where her husband is, I guess that's my brother. The woman's name is Freddie." He had to grit his teeth because it was hurting that bad now.

The cop must have thought Jjaks was in shock because he looked at him and asked, "Wait a minute, there was a woman there?"

"No . . . wait . . ." All of a sudden he didn't want to tell them anything about Freddie. "No, there wasn't a woman. And, I think my brother's dead."

A nurse had started to cut Jjaks' shirt, scissoring the thing off in about ten seconds and then telling Jjaks, "I'm going to give you a shot." She was a pretty young black girl. Jjaks could smell her perfume when she bent over him with the needle.

Behind her, the cop asked again, "Was there a woman there when you got shot or not?"

Jjaks was starting to feel a little warmer already. He mumbled, "No, earlier, she was in earlier, with a black blouse on. She got married yesterday or maybe the day before, and then she came and lived with me." He was drifting now.

The cop asked, "What kind of car was he driving?"

"Who?"

"The guy who shot you."

Jjaks wondered if they were joking. Didn't they know? "For Christ's sake, a cop car. What do you think I've been telling you?"

He heard a familiar voice, somebody saying he was in charge. Then Detective Gold leaned over him. "What'd you do with the lieutenant and the woman, Jjaks? Where'd you leave them?"

It took a long time for Jjaks to get that one. He had to struggle, think it through, and finally come up with the answer. "I didn't do anything." He was proud of the answer. His eyes kept closing and he was having trouble opening them again.

He looked up at the nurse, saw there was another man beside her now, a doctor. "How's it look?"

The nurse said, "You'll live."

Jjaks tried grinning, giving it an effort. "Ain't that a blast."

206

WHEN JJAKS woke up he knew where he was. He took one look around and everything came rushing back. He was in a bed, on a thin mattress. His back hurt in a couple of places and there was a tube going into his right arm, just below his elbow. He was surrounded by cornstalk-green walls and the smell of antiseptic, piss, and body odor.

There was a curtain on one side of the bed, preventing him from seeing half the room. From the other side of the curtain came a steady, low-pitched moan of somebody in pain.

There was something wrong with his vision. If he looked closely at anything, it swam in and out of focus. He tried shutting one eye and then the other. That seemed to help. There was a pain in his side that got worse the longer he was awake, a dull throbbing that seemed to take on the quality of a rusted knife blade, stuck in his side, jagged and burning.

He closed his eyes, tried to go back to sleep, but wasn't able to. Hell, a lifetime had happened in the last few days. The last thing he remembered was being on the floor of the motel office, watching Costikyan and Freddie disappear out the front door and then the steady high-low sound of approaching sirens. He'd passed out just as the first cops burst through the door.

The curtain was pulled aside suddenly, startling him. For an instant he expected to see Costikyan's ugly face, or Sammy's. But then he realized Sammy was dead and the lieutenant was probably long gone. It was a doctor, a man in a white lab coat who came in and took hold of Jjaks' arm. He didn't say anything as he checked Jjaks' pulse. When he was done, he turned and said to someone behind him, "A few minutes, that's all."

It was Detective Lloyd Gold. Jjaks wondered what the hell did this guy want? Any partner of Costikyan's was bound to be as fucked up as the lieutenant. Jjaks turned his head away and wouldn't look at the man. What was the point? There were bars on the window just a few feet from the bed. The cop must've been watching him. "That's right, Jjaks, you're in prison."

"I don't have to be a brain surgeon to figure that one out on my own."

"Your brother's dead. I guess you know that too?"

"Yeah." He remembered Sammy lying on the floor and Costikyan holding Sammy's nose and mouth shut to finish him off.

Detective Gold said, "For your miserable sake, I was hoping you might have an idea. See . . . we know you killed your brother. . . ."

"I didn't kill anyone."

The detective was silent for a minute and then nodded. "Maybe you did, maybe you didn't. The thing is, some of the pieces don't fit. I get a knot in my stomach, a feeling that tells me Freddie and the lieutenant might be able to fill in the blanks, tell me what happened in that office. But . . . I've got to find them first."

Jjaks laughed harshly. It hurt like hell, but he didn't care. "They got away? I guess it's only fitting."

"They're missing. They have to be located, that's all."

"Missing? Detective . . . whatever your name is . . ."

"Gold, Lloyd Gold."

"Well, Detective Gold Lloyd Gold, they aren't missing. They took off. If you were any kind of cop, you'd know that."

"If that's the case, we'll catch up to them sooner or later."

Jjaks stared at the man with contempt. Inside of himself, all he felt was despair. The cop could sit there all day and talk about catching up to people, but Jjaks had been down this way before. He knew how it worked. The cops, the DA, all they were interested in was putting somebody behind bars. It didn't matter a fuck who it was.

He said to Lloyd Gold, "You're going to hunt them down, like in that old show. Get them if it takes years?"

"We're pursuing that course of action, yes."

Jjaks said, "Jesus, save me from people like you," and turned back toward the wall. He heard the detective leave. He moved slowly on the bed, trying to find some position that helped with the pain. It was hopeless. He ended up with the pillow scrunched against his belly and his face inches from the wall. Stayed like that until the doctor came in later to check his pulse again. If he'd had the energy, he might have cried. Thinking about it, he decided, what would be the point?

―――

FREDDIE COULD see, across the desert, the faint neon glow of Las Vegas. A place of life, on an otherwise dreadfully arid landscape, holding out a promise of hope and excitement. She was that close to it. Yet it seemed to her that maybe she'd never get there.

She was in a shitty little motel room in a two-light town ten miles east of the city, off Interstate 15. If she walked outside, she could see mountains in the distance and miles of red-rock desert. There were planes overhead every couple of minutes, coming in from the east, screaming low over the desert like huge birds, and landing at McCarrin International Airport. It was the closest she had ever gotten to the place of her dreams. The land of neon, stars, and fancy cars. Glittering lights and the shiny, clinking sounds of money in slot machines. Dreamy nights.

Behind her, on the bed, Costikyan slumbered in an alcoholic stupor, the smell of his body and breath almost overwhelming. He'd gotten back just after midnight and collapsed on the mattress.

All she'd said to him when he stumbled in was, "How much?"

He was drunk, but tried to lie. "How much what?"

"Shit, how much this time? You play craps or roulette?"

He mumbled, "Craps. I was up eleven grand."

"What were you up when you walked out?"

"The fucking dice . . ." Then he'd gone into the bathroom and threw up. He stank and had little pieces of vomit on his chin. She had to look away or she'd be sick too.

That had been hours ago. The sky in the east was starting to turn pink. In fifteen minutes the desert would be as bright as in the middle of the afternoon.

She looked again at the slob on the bed. What a pig. Lieutenant Ben Costikyan. A police officer with foul breath and body odor who had trouble getting it up and had gambled away half the money they had in the last three days.

She walked over to the bed. Stood there, looking down at the sleeping figure, and then spit on his face. He didn't even move.

There was a round cloth bag by the door, with two plastic handles at the top, an oversized pocketbook. It contained all her possessions in the world. She walked over and picked it up. Costikyan stirred slightly and she froze, waited for his breathing to even out again before she opened the door. She stood for a moment, feeling the early-morning heat burn into her body. Without thinking, she put her hand to her throat and touched the locket around her neck.

She closed the door softly, walked down the sidewalk past the swimming pool, and stopped at a pay phone outside the front office. She dug a quarter out of her pocket and dialed a number. When she got through she said, "I want to speak to Detective Lloyd Gold." The person on the other end started to talk. She interrupted him. "I want to talk to Lloyd. No one else. Tell him it's Freddie calling. He'll take the call."

When she got off the phone she walked into the lobby of the motel. There was a clerk behind the desk and she went over to him and smiled sweetly. "I'm here to get . . . to get my husband's bag."

The clerk looked at her as if he knew she wasn't married to Costikyan. He shook his head. "The man said, no one touches that bag but him."

"Is that a fact," Freddie said. She peered at the man's neck. "Why, I do believe that's a new tie. Is it?"

He blushed. "Yes, as a matter of fact . . ."

She touched it, let her hands linger on the material. "I like it."

"You do?"

"It's very distinguished looking."

He looked pleased, but red enough in the face now that she thought he was going to pop.

She worked on keeping an innocent, naive expression on her face. "Well, it's the silliest thing. My husband, you met him. It's his birthday and I thought, well, I need to get him something. It's a surprise. But I need the bag."

The clerk frowned. "I have my instructions."

Freddie said, "Shit." She put her hand over her mouth. "Excuse me, but what am I going to do? I have to get it because I have a doctor's appointment in an hour." She took a step back so that the clerk could see her legs, leaned down slowly, pulling up the hem of her skirt until most of her thigh was exposed. "I have this rash, can you see it?" She looked up. "Right there, isn't it awful?"

He got redder. Freddie thought he might have a heart attack. He said, "It looks fine to me."

Freddie pushed her skirt down, stuck her lower lip out a little, and said softly, "But if I have a doctor's appointment in a little while and I have to get that bag, how in the world am I going to do that? I can't wake up my husband." She dug in her purse and pulled out a hundred-dollar bill. "Unless . . ."

She watched the expression on his face change. Finally he whispered, "Well . . . perhaps, just this once."

And she knew she was in.

FREDDIE WALKED out to the highway, hiked her skirt up again, stuck her thumb out, and got a ride in under five minutes. A trucker, driving a semi up from Tulsa, Oklahoma, pulled over and helped her up into the cab. Took his time about it, copping a feel as he held the door for her. She didn't mind at all.

He asked her, "Well, little lady, where you headed?"

She pointed toward Las Vegas. "You see that?"

"What? The Strip?"

She shook her head. "No, that's not the Strip." She thought of all the money in her purse, sixty-eight thousand dollars that Costikyan hadn't managed to gamble away. More money than she'd ever seen. It would carry her for a long time.

The trucker asked, "What do you mean, that's not the Strip? That's Vegas, honey. Anybody'd know that."

"Maybe to you it is. But to me"—she took a deep breath—"to me, that's paradise."

COSTIKYAN WOKE with a killing hangover. When he realized Freddie and her things were gone, he pulled a pair of pants on and stormed down to the motel lobby. The manager was behind the desk. There was a clerk next to him, a young guy who looked at Costikyan with a worried expression on his face.

Costikyan was yelling before he got to the front desk. "Where the hell is she?"

The manager looked surprised. "I'm sorry, sir?"

"Where the hell is she? Freddie? Where'd she go?" A thought occurred to him. "Where the hell is my bag?" Behind him he heard a familiar voice and two men in state-trooper uniforms grabbed his arms. They turned him so that he was looking into the eyes of his old partner, Detective Lloyd Gold.

"*Lloyd.*"

212

Gold had Ben's motel registration form in his hand. He glanced at it and then said, "Mr. Brown, huh? Very original."

Costikyan glanced at the front door of the lobby. There were two more state troopers there. Lloyd Gold said, "I wouldn't try running, Ben. There's nowhere to go."

"Run? What're you doing here? Why would I run? I'm on vacation. Nothing happened to my wife, did it?"

"Your wife's fine, Ben, although she's a little pissed off at you. We got a call from Freddie telling us where you were."

"Freddie? You mean Clayton?"

"And, she said some very interesting things that we think we can substantiate."

"Like what?"

"Like you're the one who actually killed Sam Clayton."

"You're gonna believe her over me? I mean, she stole all my fucking money, ask this guy right here. Tell this fucker, who works for me, that she stole every last fucking cent of mine. Go on, tell him. Look, we're cops, Lloyd, we stick together, that's what we do. If we don't look out for each other, who else will?"

One of the state troopers handcuffed Costikyan's hands behind his back. Lloyd grabbed him above the elbow, turned him, and said from a foot away, "Lemme ask you something, Ben. Why are you such a fucking dickweed? Were you born this way or created?"

———

LLOYD GOLD came to let Jjaks out. Walked him down the long corridor from the jail into an interrogation room just off the receiving area. Jjaks had no clue what was going on. Were they filing more charges? Gold didn't say much of anything during the walk and Jjaks was uncomfortable enough, having to shuffle because his side hurt and his hands were cuffed to a belt around his waist, that he didn't ask any questions.

There was a table and a couple of chairs in the room. Gold unlocked Jjaks' hands, sat down in one chair, and pointed to another.

Gold had a folder in his hands. He put it down on the table and started to leaf through it. Jjaks remembered the time he'd been in a similar room with Lieutenant Costikyan, the big man studying a folder, informing Jjaks he was a suspect in Freddie's death, and then kicking the shit out of him. Gold didn't look like the type to do that, but you could never be sure.

Jjaks broke the silence. "What happened to the dog?"

"What about it?"

"Where is he? The puppy. What'd you guys do, take him to the kennel?"

"I took him home." There was a pause and then Gold continued, "I've got to tell you, I think you're horseshit. It doesn't matter what else I'm going to say to you. I just want you to know where we stand."

"You bring me up here to call me names?"

"I brought you up here to tell you we've moved ahead in the case, got some things to tell you. But, right up front, I want you to know that I don't like you. You just got out of jail a few weeks ago and it took you all of a few days to land in a world of trouble. I think that says something about you."

Jjaks said, "You're going to kick me out of the Boy Scout troop, Detective? Is that what this is?"

"You got an answer for everything, Jjaks?"

"No, I'm just tired of it all. You motherfuckers want to play your games, pin things on me that you've got to realize I didn't do. That doesn't mean I have to play along while you get off on putting me back in prison."

"We're not putting you in prison."

It took a moment to sink in. Jjaks had to run the words over in his head again. He said slowly, "You want to say that again?"

214

"I've got a memo here from the DA's office." Gold held up the folder. "Says that as of today, all charges against you are being dropped."

"This a joke?"

"No joke. We . . . I . . . got a tip . . . a phone call that led me right to where Lieutenant Costikyan was sleeping off what looked like a weeklong drunk. We picked him up, matched ballistics with his weapon. Compared the bullet that killed your brother. And, what do you know, you didn't kill Sammy after all."

"You got a phone call?"

"That's right."

"Freddie . . . did she call?"

"I'm not discussing that with you. I thought you had the right to know, that's all."

"Was Freddie there?"

"You can go. I brought your dog in with me. He's in the other room. You can take him with you."

Jjaks wanted to grab the cop, smack him around until he told him everything. Instead, he said, "Come on, Detective. Cut me a break. You can tell me. Was she there?"

Gold seemed to reach a personal decision, because he shook his head and said, "No, there wasn't any sign of the woman. As far as we're concerned, we aren't looking for her anyway. That goes for you too. You're free to go, but if I were you, I'd find another part of the country to call home." He took two steps out into the hallway and then came back, stared hard at Jjaks, and said, "Bakersfield."

"What?"

"Bakersfield. That's where they picked up the lieutenant. A small town about ten miles east of Las Vegas, south of Nellis Air Force Base. I could be wrong, but maybe you do have a right to know."

Chapter 17

THE DRESSING ROOM WAS packed. Girls, most of them half-naked, were hurrying everywhere. There was a feel to the air, anticipation and excitement. Five minutes to show time.

Freddie was sitting in front of a long mirror, wearing a G-string and a headdress with long, brilliant green peacock feathers trailing to the floor. She checked her face in the mirror and dabbed on more lipstick.

She was nervous but had a feeling in the pit of her stomach that she was about to do the most wonderful thing in the world. She said it to herself, softly. "*Vegas.*" It sounded good.

Freddie stood outside the front door of the building before she'd gone in, savoring the feeling. A sign up top said CAESARS. Below, in bold letters, the marquee announced Julio Iglesias. Unbelievable. She'd wondered, was this a world's record, coming from Minnesota, dancing in dive bars, to, only a week later, dancing in a show at Las Vegas?

Should it be in that book, *Guinness World Records?* Maybe not. Could be all that mattered was that life might be better from now on.

She stuck a pastie on her breast and it fell off. She tried again with the same result and started to curse because there wasn't much time. Next to her, an older girl, a veteran, saw what she was trying to do, leaned over, and picked up the pastie. "Let me show you."

The girl licked the pastie and stuck it on Freddie's tit like it was the most natural thing in the world to do, and then smiled. "First night?"

"It is. I'm excited."

"That's nice." She went back to her mirror, but added, "You'll be fine. Welcome to Las Vegas."

Freddie checked out her own reflection. She had to admit, she looked pretty good. "Thanks."

She glanced at her arm where she'd had the tattoo changed. The first thing she'd done, after getting a place to stay, was to go out and have it changed. Turned it into a flower that covered up the word *slut*. Even from up close, no one could tell it had ever been anything different.

The last thing she did, before filing out with the rest of the women to go on stage, was pick up the gold chain from the counter and place it carefully around her neck. She only had a moment to sit in front of the mirror, watching the heart on the end of the chain catch the light and sparkle.

That woman was right. She was going to be just fine.

―――

JJAKS STUCK his thumb out on Boulder Highway. The dog sat quietly by his feet until they got picked up by a trucker carrying a load of Bibles out to a church in Las Vegas.

"Where ya headed?" the trucker asked.

"Vegas."

"You ain't going out there to gamble? I can't abide folks that gamble."

"Not me, I don't believe in it. You work too hard for what you got, no sense throwin' it away." He repeated the words softly. "No, sir, you work too hard to throw it away."

The trucker nodded and put his rig in gear. "That's a nice dog you got." A few minutes later he said, "Fellow like you, you might want to carry a Bible with you."

"Bible?"

"Can't tell when you might feel the urge to read the Good Book. I got a whole load of them. I could let you have one for five bucks." He reached behind him, pulled a new Bible from behind the seat, and said, "The Good Book. That's what I sell."

Jjaks reached into his pocket. There was a letter in there, a short note that he'd gotten from Freddie just before he got out of jail. It was written on lined notebook paper, opened and refolded dozens of times. "Thanks, but the truth is, I got everything I need to read right here."

"What's that?"

"It's a love letter."

"Yeah?"

Jjaks began to read. " 'Dear Jjaks.' That's me. 'Maybe it's all bullshit, maybe nothing does happen for a reason after all. But I'm doing great, I'm living my dreams. So, fuck you anyway. Freddie.' " Jjaks glanced up at the trucker and smiled. "You see what I mean? I got all the reading I need. Right here." He folded up the letter and stuck it back into his pocket.

The driver was silent for another couple of miles and then he said, "Pal, I got to tell you something. I hope you don't take offense and it ain't any of my business. But I'm a Christian man and I got to say, that don't sound like any kind of love letter to me."

Jjaks let the man finish before he started to laugh. When

218

he finally stopped, the driver was looking at him like he wasn't sure Jjaks was sane. He said. "What you laughing at?"

"You don't think this is a love letter?"

"Didn't sound like it to me."

In front of him Jjaks could see the Strip of Vegas. Caesars Palace was visible just ahead. "All you got to do, you get a letter like this, you got to read between the lines." He picked up his small bag from the seat next to him and petted the dog. "You can let me off anywhere up here."

"Anywhere?"

"Yeah." He pulled a cigarette out of his pocket, flipped it up toward his mouth, and caught it in his teeth in one easy motion. Took a deep breath of the desert air, thinking of Freddie up ahead, and said, "Don't you worry about me. I know where I'm going."

FINE LINE FEATURES PRESENTS A JERSEY FILMS PRODUCTION

A FILM BY STEVEN BAIGELMAN

KEANU REEVES

"FEELING MINNESOTA"

VINCENT D'ONOFRIO CAMERON DIAZ DELROY LINDO

COURTNEY LOVE WITH TUESDAY WELD

AND DAN AYKROYD

MUSIC SUPERVISOR KARYN RACHTMAN CASTING DIRECTOR FRANCINE MAISLER

COSTUME DESIGN EUGENIE BAFALOUKOS PRODUCTION DESIGNER NAOMI SHOHAN

EDITOR MARTIN WALSH DIRECTOR OF PHOTOGRAPHY WALT LLOYD

ASSOCIATE PRODUCER CARLA SANTOS-MACY CO-PRODUCER ERIC McLEOD

EXECUTIVE PRODUCER ERWIN STOFF PRODUCED BY DANNY DeVITO

MICHAEL SHAMBERG STACEY SHER

WRITTEN AND DIRECTED BY STEVEN BAIGELMAN

SOUNDTRACK ALBUM AVAILABLE ON ATLANTIC RECORDS

A division of New Line Cinema